DR. Z AND MATTY TAKE TELEGRAPH

ARI ROSENSCHEIN

ISBN: 979-8-88653-227-2

Fire & Ice Young Adult Books
An Imprint of Melange Books, LLC
White Bear Lake, MN 55110
www.fireandiceya.com

Published in the United States of America.

Cover Design by Ashley Redbird Designs

As with everything I write, Dr. Z and Matty Take Telegraph is dedicated to Adrienne, Arlo, and Lucca. In addition, many thanks to the close friends I've been lucky to have in my life and who course through the veins of this book. Whether or not we're in touch, our shared pain, laughter, and obsessions form the story's emotional core. You know who you are, and I celebrate you with these words.

Many thanks to my trusted readers, Tim Cummings and Meg Gaertner, for their early support and feedback. I also extend gratitude to Adrienne Pierce for continuity tips and character insights, Eric Shea for skate specifics and East Bay lore, Jo Townson for Berkeley details, and John Getze for making the game of water polo come alive in these pages.

This book includes excerpts from the following public-domain works: "I meant to have but modest needs" by Emily Dickinson, "In Cabin'd Ships at Sea" by Walt Whitman, and "Side by Side" by Thomas Hardy.

PRAISE FOR DR. Z AND MATTY TAKE TELEGRAPH

"Rife with all the crackle of skate culture—the lingo, the clothing, the music—Rosenschein's YA debut is a kickflip, a deeply impactful exploration of the mercurial nature of male friendship, of family, mental affliction, and finally, transformation. Imagine a mash-up between *A Separate Peace*, *Lords of Dogtown*, and a John Hughes movie scored by Bad Religion and A Tribe Called Quest, and you're halfway there."

—TIM CUMMINGS, BEST-SELLING
AUTHOR OF *ALICE THE CAT*

"*Dr. Z and Matty Take Telegraph* is a keenly and compassionately observed coming-of-age story that glows with truth and yearning. Reading this book feels the way falling in love and making a new best friend alight on the young and hungry heart."

—JEFF ZENTNER, AWARD-WINNING
AUTHOR OF *IN THE WILD LIGHT*

"Expertly crafted throughout, *Dr. Z and Matty Take Telegraph* captures the pure sunlight and uncertainty of California and coming of age, from the bright moments to the blind spots, from what is illuminated to what the radiance obscures."

—STACY D. FLOOD, AUTHOR OF *THE SALT FIELDS*

"*Dr. Z and Matty Take Telegraph* is a musical journey through adolescence. I thoroughly enjoyed the late-'90s nostalgia. Rosenschein does a great job of portraying the impact of the people we surround ourselves with and how these relationships shape us, for better or worse."

—AUTUMN LINDSEY, AUTHOR OF *REMAINING AILEEN*

"In *Dr. Z and Matty Take Telegraph*, Ari Rosenschein pulls us back to the East Bay Area college town's pre-internet 1990s without succumbing to the trappings of nostalgia. Winding through a colorful backdrop of gritty subculture and analog academia, this charming book introduces complex personalities who traverse the tragedies and triumphs of adolescence."

—ERIC SHEA, AUTHOR OF *LIVING MOD: BERKELEY IN THE 1980S*

"*Dr. Z and Matty Take Telegraph* immersed me in a world heady with the symphony of the teenage experience. The book is a sensitive look at the impacts of mental health and how music can help us connect and see the best in each other."

—MIREYA SERRANO VELA, AUTHOR OF
VESTIGES OF COURAGE

"*Dr. Z and Matty Take Telegraph* perfectly captures the tremulous passage of time, where teenagers often find themselves—that last spurt of internal growth before entering young adulthood. Ari Rosenschein has crafted a beautiful novel, especially for those young readers who are struggling to embrace the flux of change that, in the end, rewards us all."

— PATRICK O'NEIL, AUTHOR OF
ANARCHY AT THE CIRCLE K

CONTENTS

ONE
THE UNKNOWN WORLD

It's as good a day as any to leave our past in the dust. Mom swears this move to Berkeley is gonna be a fresh start for both of us, but for me, it's more like a shot at a new identity. As we speed down the highway, I feel a growing distance from Dad, my parent's divorce, and everything else—but mostly from my old self.

We started our road trip bright and early in Tempe with milkshake sugar buzzes and just crash-landed at a Travelodge in Riverside with sun headaches and gas station food bellies.

"Your father would've done the whole drive in one shot," Mom says, slamming the trunk of our Acura Integra.

She's right. The entire trip should only take about twelve hours, but Mom decided to break it up into two days.

I'm already dragging my suitcase towards the beckoning lights of the motel. "Let's not talk about that guy," I yell over my shoulder, but the wheels on gravel drown me out. As far as Dad is concerned, he can stay in the desert—Scottsdale, Santa Fe, wherever his wanderlust leads him. He made his choices, now he has to live with them.

Outside the Travelodge lobby, under fluorescent bulbs in the balmy early evening, I wait while Mom gets our keys from the night staff. By the time our room greets us with crisp sheets, a Pine-Sol-fresh bathroom, and loud air-conditioning, I'm ready to pass out. The last thing I remember before I drop dead is Mom's voice asking the front desk about a wake-up call.

When I eventually awaken, it's morning, but you wouldn't know it from our pitch-black room. I slept right through the phone ringing. I roll out of bed, pull on some gym shorts and a tank top, and lace up my dirty Nike Air Max 95s. Mom's not around, so she's feasting on the bounty of baked goods already.

Since there's some privacy, I lift my shirt in front of the full-length motel mirror. This is a ritual for when I'm alone, but Mom's caught me a few times. My sixteenth birthday passed in July, but the broad shoulders and muscle gains from wrestling last year make people think I'm older. Though most of the time, I still feel like a kid in my head.

Right now, I'm hoping my reflection will reassure me. Nope. Pecs, delts, and biceps are acceptable but nowhere near where I want them to be. As soon as I started lifting in eighth grade gym class, it became an obsession. Coincidentally, that was when Mom and Dad split up.

The mirror also reveals that my hair is most definitely not happening. I've been letting my freshman flattop grow out this summer, so brown tufts are sticking out in half a dozen directions. It does this when I don't tame it down with gel. Whatever. There's no one at the Travelodge to impress.

Standing in the breakfast line makes me remember all the good times the Tempe High wrestling team had during out-of-town tournaments. Beds we didn't have to make, cable TV, and all the orange juice and muffins we could eat.

This trip is different. It almost feels like we're escaping rather than moving to a new state. Maybe we are.

Turns out I was wrong about there being no one to impress at the motel. A few tables over, I see a family of five with three kids. Two of them are misbehaving twins, and the third is a tall redhead in a pink sweatsuit who looks about my age. She catches me looking but turns away. I push my hair down. Damn it. Should have worn something cooler.

After loading up my breakfast plate, I pick a table. While shoveling food in my mouth with one hand, I open *The Invisible Man* by H.G. Wells, a book on the Berkeley High tenth-grade summer reading list. That's one valuable thing Dad taught me; always be in a book.

"Six hours until we begin our new existence, kiddo," Mom says, interrupting my reading. She's returned with a plate piled high with thick pancakes, fluffed-up eggs, and buttery toast.

"That's a bold statement." I flip a page.

Mom licks some jam from her index finger. "Well, fortune favors the bold."

"Who's bold in this scenario?" I say extra loud. Hopefully, the redhead hears and is dazzled by my maturity.

"You and me, buddy. You and me." She notices the family of five. "Has someone captured my angst-ridden son's attention?"

"Jeez, Mom. Could you broadcast that to the whole room?"

"Sorry, sorry."

She digs into her food, and I am grateful for the quiet so I can try to catch the redhead's eye again between snippets of H.G. Wells. No success. You see, I'm a hopeless romantic, prone to falling in love several times a day, an hour even. I've also never had a real girlfriend except for Janie Mullins at Archery camp the summer before seventh grade. She broke it off before school started—said I was too needy.

Mom scoots her seat back. "You ready to hit the road?"

"Yup, time to meet the left-wing radicals in Cali."

"Zack, all kinds of people live in Berkeley."

"You know that was only to rile you up."

My eighth-grade history teacher told our class that Berkeley was "home to more nutsos per capita than anywhere in the US." He followed that nugget up by saying he expected many of us would end up there. Needless to say, both my liberal parents disagreed with his curriculum, especially the gung-ho way he taught us about the Vietnam War and how much he praised Ronald Reagan.

I stand and push my chair in, stretch my arms over my head to show off some muscle tone, and shoot the redheaded girl one last hopeful look as we walk out. We're ships in the night, as I head off into the unknown world known as The Golden State.

Today is all cloudless blue skies and dried-up farmland. The Cali highway is drab compared to Arizona's crimson rock formations and towering cacti. Mom is rapping along to "Wannabe" by the Spice Girls—not my favorite song in the world.

With a leg on the dashboard, I crack open *The Invisible Man*, turning pages with one hand and lifting my trusty ten-pound dumbbell with the other. Deviating from my exercise routine freaks me out.

Mom turns the radio down just as ads start to invade the car. "I hope you're not too bummed out by your new school's lack of decent wrestling."

"It'll be fine."

"I know it's an adjustment on top of an adjustment. Another example of how mature you are."

"Whatever you say, Mom." Who knows? Maybe I'll be like "the stranger" in Wells's novel: the new guy everyone tries to figure out. A mystery man. Dad for sure saw himself that way —an outlaw intellectual with a poetry book, the guy who read me excerpts from *The Prince* by Machiavelli as a bedtime story.

Not that the apple fell too far from the tree; I'm pretty reclusive. Back home, people knew me as a good wrestler and student, but I never let anyone get too close. I had plenty of acquaintances but no best buddies or even a friend group. Maybe I've got trust issues or something.

After an hour of reading and lifting, I grow nauseous, and I drop H.G. into the black hole between the seat and the door. "Doesn't it feel weird that we've never been inside our new house?"

Mom turns the radio down. She's gone quiet, which means my question irked her. In the two years since Dad bailed on us, I've perfected the art of getting under her skin. I'm not proud of this ability—just good at it.

"The HR woman from the university swears the neighborhood is fabulous." Some frizzy hair escapes from behind her ear, and she pushes it back. "They always set up housing for new professors and their families."

"Our family of *two*, you mean."

Mom turns the radio back up, louder now. The signal is crackly—we've lost the station. A few minutes pass. "And just so you aren't disappointed, remember, it's an apartment, not a house. That's what we could afford in the Berkeley market."

"Doesn't 'apartment' mean we're downgrading?"

She ignores me and scans the dial. "Looks like we're in a dead zone. Do we need to go over why we're moving again?"

"Only if you want to, Mom."

"Opportunities like this for female professors don't come along often—"

"You've told me."

"I'll have a chance at tenure," she continues like she's rehearsing in the mirror. "UC Berkeley holds real weight in the world of academia. Plus, we both need a more enlightened environment." She cranks the AC. "I sure do."

"Mom, like I've said ten million times, I'm just as happy to get away from Arizona as you are. Too many memories—mostly bad ones."

"I love these lyrics," Mom says, changing the subject. And away she goes, bellowing off-key while patting the steering wheel to "If It Makes You Happy." After stopping for a Slurpee in Bakersfield, I pass out to the sound of her humming along to "Macarena." God, that song is horrible.

I emerge from my car nap sweaty and dazed, with my head pressed against the window. The late-day rays warm my forehead as I sit up. Between sips of warm Slurpee, I watch two Porsches pass us. "California plates."

Mom smiles like I'm coming around to her plan at last.

TWO
WELCOME TO BERZERKELEY

Traffic thickens as we approach civilization, and the hills are transformed on either side of the freeway. No more endless brown. Now everything is a sea of green bushes and trees, and even the sunlight feels a tad softer, like it's tinted with copper. It's also a bit foggier than I expected here. Guess that's what it's like close to the San Francisco Bay.

After two days on the road, we reach our exit. Talk about instant culture shock; the first thing I see are joggers in blue and yellow University of California Berkeley sweatshirts hopping over a panhandler in tie-dyed sweatpants.

"Get a load of this guy," I say, tapping the window. "He looks like he thinks it's 1967 instead of '97."

"Let's practice some tolerance, Zack."

"I haven't seen this many dancing bear T-shirts in my life. For real."

"Berkeley is a center of the progressive thought."

"And hippies."

Mom shoots me a fake glare, but she seems genuinely happy, which makes me optimistic. It's been a tough couple of years for her—for both of us—with the divorce. But it wasn't always bad.

My parents met in the late '70s as undergrads at Arizona State. They were birds of a feather: intellectual academics in rough-and-tumble Tempe. Mom was a brilliant up-and-coming biochemistry researcher, and Dad was an English professor who lived for poetry. Both ended up pursuing advanced degrees and teaching at ASU. Oh, and at some point I showed up. Flash-forward sixteen years, and here we are. Except we're missing one crucial family member: Dad.

Mom honks the horn. "Eat shit, buddy," she says, raising a middle finger toward the offending Toyota Camry.

"Oops, that's one for the swear jar," I say, even though our family's never been strict about language.

"Well, you can eat shit, too. Did you see him pull that California Stop?"

"What even *is* a California Stop?"

She makes a wide right turn. "Pausing at a stop sign without bringing the car to a full halt."

"So, it's an official DMV thing?" I've been studying for my permit, and this sounds like something that could be on a test.

"I'm not sure. But it's very irritating."

At first, we pass some houses with nice lawns and kids running through sprinklers. This looks like a more upscale version of our Tempe neighborhood. Maybe all college areas feel identical.

Then, after a few blocks, the number of apartment buildings increases, and so does the city vibe until, without warning, we reach our new home: a three-story, wood-paneled complex more or less the color of diarrhea. The moving van Mom hired in Arizona is taking up at least three spots in front.

Mom parks the Acura, and we stand for the first time in

hours. Thank God for a chance to flex my muscles. The air is sweet in this new city, like a car freshener minus the headache. "California smells different."

Mom smiles. "Jasmine." She extends her sun-freckled arms as if to capture the scent. "Not bad, huh?"

She takes a few woozy steps in the direction of the apartments, my science professor hippie mother in her summer uniform of a tie-dye T-shirt and loose jog string pants.

"Well, I'm not going to complain about the weather. Tempe is an oven in late August."

Each apartment has a small outdoor area, and they're all jammed full of plants, bicycles, and multi-colored prayer flags. The place looks like a yoga center or something and is a definite step down from our Tempe house, which had neat rock landscaping and a two-car garage.

Of course, there's no reason to verbalize these first impressions. Why spoil the mood by saying something snarky? Mom deserves to bathe in her sense of accomplishment.

Now she's crossing the street, Birkenstocks slapping against the concrete, hair bouncing like cotton candy. My mom looks at ease already, almost like this new life was right here all along, just waiting for her.

"You want to see the inside?" she asks. "We'll take a quick peek, then run back and meet the mover."

Mom leads the way through a courtyard and opens a wooden gate to our new place. "Told you we got a floor unit," she says, waving a glinting, never-before-used golden key and unlocking the door.

"Only like twenty times."

We enter the apartment, and its utter emptiness hits me. Beige carpet, cream walls, squeaky-clean bathtubs. No familiar knickknacks or cozy clutter, none of Mom's science journals or Dad's poetry books. It's neither new nor old. It's neither tiny nor big. And it's certainly not a home, more like a box without personality.

"Wait until we put our stamp on this place," Mom says, as if she read my mind. "Get all your wrestling posters and trophies out."

"It's fine, Mom. I'll get used to it."

My parents sold the Arizona house as part of their divorce terms, and my mom got full custody. They explained everything to me during one of our last talks as a family. We were sitting on the living room couch in Tempe when they made the whole thing final—me situated directly between them, like a buffer.

It took forever to find a buyer, so Mom and I stayed at the house up through the beginning of freshman year when she rented a smaller place. Somewhere in there, Dad went off to find himself, and I haven't talked to him in around two years. These days, Dad is a ghost to me who Mom refers to as "Silas" or "your father."

Squinting away memories, I follow Mom back to the truck—no point living in the past. A lean guy in paint-splattered jeans and a Phoenix Suns shirt steps out from the cab. This is who my Mom hired to move us. He's got sunburned skin that looks like it's pulling his face tight. I watch as he unlatches the rear door.

"Let me help," I say.

"Have at it." Our mover sounds like he took bong rips the entire drive here.

He hands me a lamp, and after two long days in the car, I'm happy to get a workout in. Dashing back and forth between the truck and the apartment is the perfect chance. It's a minor thrill beating the mover 5-3 in number of trips; nothing gets my blood pumping like some competition.

Once we're down to the last few items, the stoned mover

sets a box marked "Sports Trophies" on the floor with a groan, like he's out of gas. Zack for the win.

Mover dude wipes his forehead and straightens himself. "I'll leave the last couple of boxes in the living room. That work for you?"

Mom looks up from an old yearbook of mine. "Oh, anywhere is fine." She hands him an envelope full of cash. "Safe driving. It's a long trek back."

"Will do," the dude says, then pockets the bills and leaves. Suddenly, it's just my mom and me in California—like it will be until I graduate from high school.

"No offense, but that guy looks like he dropped out in seventh grade."

"That's quite judgmental of you." Mom rips the masking tape from another box. "You come from an educated family, but that's not the only barometer of success."

"Whatever. Maybe I *am* judgmental." It's not like Mom doesn't have plenty of her own biases about science, politics, and the world in general, which she is happy to share on a daily basis.

She fishes inside a cardboard box and emerges with a scratched-up gold trophy. "Remember this one?"

"Tournament in Flagstaff, I think."

"You *think*?" Mom sets the award down like an archaeological prize. We can't bullshit each other. She knows I'm obsessed with my trophies.

Exploring the place takes all of three minutes; we have two bedrooms, a common area, and a tiny kitchen. The off-white walls smell like they were painted yesterday, and unlike our adobe house in Tempe with its wall-to-wall carpeting, this place is all hardwood. It seems like somewhere college students should live, not a family home.

For a second, I try to visualize a future version of myself living here—a cool, confident city kid with places to go and people to do things with. Not an outsider with no friends, no wrestling, and no father around.

"We'll make this house a socks-only zone," Mom says as my shoes squeak on the freshly waxed floor.

"All the time?"

"What's wrong with that?" She kicks off one sandal, then the other. "It'll be very California."

I open the screen door to investigate the small outside space. It's only a few feet of concrete, but it's workable. "Can I set up my gym out here?"

"Zack, there's no need to shout." She follows me outside. "Yes, the weights can go outside."

Navigating the battlefield of boxes, I enter an empty bedroom, the smaller of the pair. It's got a mirrored closet door without a single streak and two windows. "Which one is mine?" I ask, hoping she takes the hint I'd like the other.

Mom bites her lip. "Well, this bedroom has more windows, which I prefer." She strides into the room across the hall and opens the closet door. "Yup, I'll be just fine here. You take the big one, Zack."

Score. "I'll bring in the last of your boxes."

She squeezes my arm. "My strong guy."

"C'mon, Mom." I pull away, but I'm flattered. My parents never pressured me about athletics; I pursued wrestling and weightlifting on my own. It's all part of my Renaissance man plan to cultivate the mind and the body.

I drag two overstuffed boxes marked "Margaret" into her bedroom. "Dude, what's in these?"

"*Dude*, books." Mom slides a ruler through the packing tape and pulls the flaps aside, revealing piles of college text-books: *Cellular Biology and Anatomical Sciences, Ecology and Evolutionary Biology, Genetics, Microbiology and Immunology, Pharmacology and Toxicology.*

She heaves up a volume called *Neural Science Basics* and

flips it open. "God, I haven't opened this in years," she says as I head to my new room.

Assembling my bed is a wrestling match in itself: switching positions, getting pinned, grunting back to dominance, and finally emerging victorious. Next, it's all about hanging posters, including a prized one from a Wrestle-Mania event I attended a few years back. Sure, it's immature and fake, but there's still a soft spot in my heart for professional wrestling, even as entertainment.

All that's left is to take my weights, bench, and barbell rack outside to assemble the outdoor gym. Over a neat wooden fence separating us from our neighbors, I see a guy with thinning hair and a short beard locking his front door. He notices me and walks over, resting his chin on a post.

"Moving in?"

"Yup, we're from Tempe," I say and slide a weight on the bar. "My mom is teaching at UC Berkeley."

"Makes sense. There's a slew of profs in this complex. I'm Geoff." The guy reaches out his hand. "I teach political science."

"Zack." I give him a tough-guy handshake.

"Well, Zack, welcome to Berzerkeley."

"Thanks, man." I shove a piece of cardboard under the wobbly leg of my lifting bench. Berzerkeley? Geoff tries too hard to sound cool. He also didn't need to say he was UC Berkeley faculty. Grow up around professors, and you can spot one with no trouble.

Clank. The bar comes down. Ten bench presses, probably too fast, and my chest feels like it'll break from any more exertion. That's enough for today.

There's a steady stream of noise from the street: sirens, people yelling, and cars with the bass booming. Each sound is a reminder that we're not in Tempe anymore. Moving states is like interstellar travel; this city is an unfamiliar planet, and it's going to take a while to adjust to the new atmosphere.

Inside, I find Mom hunched over a dresser, absorbed in a framed picture of me, Dad, and her at the Grand Canyon in 1994. I was a thirteen-year-old twerp in a St. Bernard shirt that read, "If You Can't Fish with The Big Dogs, Stay on The Dock."

"Ancient history," I say. "But we did look pretty happy."

She brushes some dust off the frame. "Yes, we did."

That was another life—once upon a time in Tempe.

THREE
END-OF-SUMMER BUMMERS

All empty campuses have the same creepy mood—a combination of stillness and anticipation, like things are supposed to be happening that aren't. The ghosts of past graduates haunt every hall. If you squint, you can almost make out their vapors bumping into each other. Or maybe I'm being dramatic because I'm nervous about meeting with my new guidance counselor.

I crane my neck to take in the old-fashioned architecture as Mom and I walk across a sprawling plaza. "You're sure this is a high school?"

"Looks like the Academic Building over there," she says, pointing at an imposing structure.

We arrive precisely on time for my appointment. My counselor looks beamed straight out of a 1950s movie, right smack down to the old-fashioned glasses on a chain resting on her white sweater.

"How many kids go here again?" I ask, trying to drum up some enthusiasm.

"Most years, we have between 2,800 and 3,000 students."

Mom nudges me. "Pretty large student body, huh, Zack?"

Uh, major understatement. Tempe High had half that number of kids.

My guidance counselor licks her left index finger and flips through my file. "You're an athlete, I see. We've got an excellent water polo team here, the Yellowjackets."

Mom already broke the news that Berkeley High wrestling was a wash, so I'm neither surprised nor disappointed. "I'm planning to try out," I tell the counselor.

"Excellent, Zack." She holds my transcript to her nose like she's trying to determine if it's counterfeit. "From the looks of your science background, you'll be going into chemistry this year."

"Yup, chem." I notice a framed photograph of a familiar landscape on the wall behind her. "Is that Arizona?"

"Close," she says, smiling, eyes clouding. "New Mexico. But I adore Arizona, especially Sedona. The energy there is exquisite."

Exquisite energy? Well, that's the most Berzerkeley thing I've heard since we arrived, but hey, the day is still young.

"I used to go there every spring," Mom says, visibly jazzed by the Sedona connection.

"How wonderful. Did you go, Zack?"

"Nope."

"It was for a Women in Science retreat," my mother clarifies.

The counselor swivels her chair towards me. "Well, I certainly hope you go out for water polo with Coach Reardon. He's tough on the outside, but the boys all love him. Your grades and achievements make you a strong contender." She pulls on her glasses and looks me up and down. "You swim, right?"

I nod.

"And I can see you're in excellent shape."

Yuck. She must have like eight grandkids.

Mom stands and offers a hand, her mass of silver bracelets piling up at the wrist. "We appreciate your time. Thank you for such excellent suggestions."

And with that, two former Tempe residents wander out into the kind of late-summer day that makes me wish September would never come. As we stroll out, I slide my hands into the pockets of my PacSun shorts.

Just before we reach the car, I see a pair of girls on bikes. They're both wearing frayed jean shorts and flip-flops and look around my age. It's a serious struggle, but I force myself not to turn my head and follow as they bike out of view. Checking out girls while standing beside the person who gave birth to you feels plain wrong.

I climb into our car and roll down my window. One final look at Berkeley High before the first day of school and my heart flutters with that sense of possibility a new school year brings. If summer has to end for sophomore life to begin, so be it. And if water polo is the name of the game here, well, that means I have to jump in the pool.

"OK, I'm taking you shopping," Mom says.

I groan, my reverie interrupted. "But I've got clothes, Mom."

"Threadbare T-shirts with holes. You don't want to look like that at your new school."

"Got it."

"So sorry you have to go shopping. It's a rough life."

"I'm a Cancer. I like hiding inside my shell." I'm repeating verbatim something a hippie kid told me a few years back at summer camp. But why would I want to go back-to-school shopping? Back at the apartment, we have TV and a stocked fridge.

We have to drive all the way out to somewhere called

Walnut Creek to find a half-assed mall where Mom drags me through a few lackluster department stores, forcing me to try on cargo pants and polo shirts. Apparently, every high school kid in the area is also here today. With my in-between hair and lame clothes, I feel dull and small-town. Adding insult to injury, I'm like the only teenager within a three-mile radius accompanied by a parent.

She walks ahead, and I slow down to catch myself in the window of The Limited. My reflection could be worse. Sure, my hair looks pathetic, but my arms are solid, and there's a late-summer tan happening.

We pass the food court, where I stare longingly at Panda Express. I nudge my mom's shoulder, but she's distracted by her watch. "Shoot, we're supposed to meet the phone people in fifteen minutes."

Well, that means no Panda Express. Instead, I get a front-row ticket to the stressed-out parent show as she rushes back home while swearing at other drivers. It's pretty funny.

Back at the apartment (now featuring phone service like an actual home), I drag the 20-foot gray cable into my room, sit on my bed, and face the age-old question: Who is there to call? My life in Tempe was sorely lacking in tight friendships —as in, there were *none*. No one to share secrets with or do whatever buddies do. The dial tone mocks me until I settle on this guy, Miguel, a wrestling buddy I've known since middle school. He looks up to me, and I'm in the mood to brag to someone.

"Tell me about the girls in California," Miguel begs. "Are there *Baywatch* babes everywhere?"

Here's the thing. Miguel is a good guy, just painfully immature, so I humor him. "Well, I just got back from the mall, and there were tons of hotties there." My forced Cali slang makes me wince. Hopefully, that can improve with practice, like wrestling form or weightlifting techniques.

"Don't lie." Miguel snorts. "You're still hoping Madeline will wake up and figure out you're her dream guy."

Sigh. Madeline Desmond was a sweet girl with braces and a loud laugh who I pined for back in seventh grade. She developed dramatically in the summer before high school, and plenty of aspiring Romeos started horning in, leaving no room for me. Yup, I've always been a sentimental sucker.

"I think I'm ready to move on from Madeline." More like, let's switch the subject. "You must be pumped for wrestling to start."

"What am I supposed to do without you to help me train?"

"You'll do great." OK, that may be an exaggeration, but my heart is in the right place. Miguel never ranks and rarely starts—good sportsmanship, though.

I promise to call again soon, which is a lie. Then I hang up the phone and scoot against the wall so I'm beneath the gaze of my wrestling heroes. Alone, as usual. It's a feeling I used to relish, but it doesn't fit me anymore. Kind of like sneakers you once loved that are too tight in the toe. Talking to Miguel left me with a bunch of melancholy realizations.

End-of-Summer Bummer One: Starting at ground zero at Berkeley High. No grade school classmates who grew up with me. All the kids will be best friends with histories and inside jokes.

End-of-Summer Bummer Two: In Tempe, everyone knew the teachers to request and the crappy ones to avoid. Here, it's new classes, new expectations, and new stress.

End-of-Summer Bummer Three: No one here cares about my kickass athletic achievements. Not to sound stuck up, but I had a killer rep as a wrestler back home. Now, I'm a transfer student who's good at a sport Berkeley High couldn't give a rat's ass about.

This is the sort of stuff a dad is supposed to be around to

talk you through. Not that my father gave a shit about wrestling, water polo, or any other organized sport. Instead, he'd share some oddball piece of folksy wisdom, usually from a writer who died a century earlier, that would somehow set me in the right direction. A penny saved speaks louder than words, or whatever.

FOUR
MACHIAVELLIAN

It's been less than a week since we moved to Berkeley, and I'm sitting in homeroom on the first day of school. As I look around the classroom from my cracked blue plastic desk, my fellow students all appear exhausted, bored, or a combination of both. Not me. I'm a jungle cat jumping out of my skin with coiled first-day energy—a 6 a.m. workout will do that to you. Gives you that edge.

Our homeroom teacher is a guy in his twenties with a big bald spot wearing a sweater vest over a white button-up. I know the type—his first year in the classroom. He's rattling off last names like he's been waiting his whole life for the opportunity to do this.

"Campbell, Nelson."

"Present." Jock with big guns. Water polo player, maybe?

"Carter, Dominique."

"Here," answers a girl in expensive-looking sneakers and a pink sweatshirt.

"Carlson, Rebecca."

"Here," replies a future prom queen with crimped blonde hair and huge hoop earrings.

"Chang, Danny."

The voice comes from two desks to my right. Danny's wearing a Nirvana T-shirt under a beat-up leather jacket, and even lacking much weed experience, I know he's utterly blazed. At my old school, guys like him hung around the 7-11, hassling people to buy them cigarettes and beer.

"Present," Danny responds, polite as can be. My mom might be right about how judgmental I am.

"Cole, Simon."

"Present," chirps a guy in an OP sweatshirt towards the back of the room. Years of experience have taught me that the last name Cole is a signal that my number is up.

"Coleman, Zack."

"Here." My heart is thumping like a basketball, but hopefully I sound laid-back and Berkeley High-ready.

Our homeroom teacher gets through the rest of the roster, then says it's cool to socialize as long as we keep things "somewhat manageable." A bunch of kids take him up on it, primarily dudes congregating around Rebecca. "As if," I overhear her tell one overzealous bonerbrain.

Arms crossed on my cold desk, my muscles are as tense as my mood. Milling around aimlessly is not on my first-day homeroom agenda. Being the new kid in a structured situation is OK, like when there are questions on the board to answer or a lecture to take notes on. Right now, ten open minutes without a friend feels like a decade.

But a minor miracle occurs. Space cadet Danny Chang approaches my desk, smelling like a tangy combination of cigarettes, leather, and body odor.

"Are you new here? Haven't seen you before."

"Yup. I just transferred from Arizona. My mom got a job at the University of California."

Danny looks impressed. "Cal. Righteous."

"Cal?"

"You know, UC Berkeley."

Ouch. How come no one told me that's what you call the school.

"Cal's rad. It's like having an undercover party school in town," Danny informs me, glossing over my ignorance. "Unfortunately, you need killer grades to get in."

"That's what I hear."

My new friend plants himself on the vacant desktop beside me and puts both feet on the seat. Then he reaches into his jacket and taps something out of sight but likely illegal. "You smoke, dude?"

"Nah, I'm good. Water polo tryouts are coming up." It's easy to spit out an excuse when you've avoided marijuana a thousand times.

"Polo. That's sweet."

Water polo doesn't seem like Danny's thing, so I appreciate the effort. I point at his shirt. "You into music?"

"Yup," Danny says with a slow grin. "Nirvana, Blink 182, Incubus, all that kind of stuff."

In all honesty, Nirvana is just a word to me, even though I know they are like the most popular alternative rock band ever. Some people know every song and album ever recorded, whereas whatever is on the radio is fine by me. I'm out of my depth, so it's best to get off the topic. "What's your next class?"

"Geometry with Mr. Salisbury, like the steak." Danny laughs at his own joke. "You?"

"Chemistry with..." I inspect my class schedule. "...Mrs. Beamish. You know her?"

Danny never gets to answer; the passing bell rings. While its shrill tone reverberates, the classroom comes to life. Students hop up, grab backpacks, and swarm toward the door.

"Let's meet up at lunch," Danny says, after we finally make it outside. "I'll find you in the cafeteria."

My judgmental asshole side warns me about aligning with such a prominent stoner in a brand-new school environment, while my practical side reminds me that it's always better to have company. Yet with those simple words, he relieved me of a lingering fear: eating alone on the first day of my tenth-grade California life.

"Sweet," I reply.

As I wander the halls between classes, I see how vastly different the racial makeup of Berkeley High is from my old school. Tempe High was majority Hispanic, but there are way more African American and Asian students here. The vibe is diverse and bustling—like a self-contained city of teenagers. I feel more worldly already.

The first half of the day rips by without anything particularly horrible happening. Almost every teacher seems inexperienced and overwhelmed, and they all spend their whole period covering class expectations. The exception is English, where I feel like a superstar right out of the gate.

Our teacher, Mrs. Garcia, is stern but cool and treats us like adults. She doesn't mind if kids cuss if we stay on topic, and she puts us to work, making us write an in-class essay on *The Invisible Man*. Luckily, that's no sweat since I'm done with that book and already deep into *A Raisin in the Sun*, which the class won't even read for a few months. Based on the moaning sounds of my classmates, I'm in the minority of people who completed the summer reading.

As the lunch bell hits, it takes all my focus to get from point A to point B without freaking out. In every direction, waves of students envelop me—jocks, hippies, gamers, cheerleaders. The cliques are so defined that the whole school feels like a massive dress-up party I wasn't invited to.

Girls are huddled in packs with immaculate makeup and

pressed miniskirts, dudes are chilling in expensive sneakers and jeans that sag effortlessly, and sockless preppies roam around like they rule the school. They all skip, laugh, and shove like they know their exact place in the ecosystem. It's like I've landed in *Clueless.*

As promised, Danny finds me in the cafeteria line at lunch. While we wait, he receives a nonstop stream of kids walking up, high-fiving him, asking, "What's up?"

"Looks like the whole school knows you, man." I slide my tray down the silver holder, eyeing the lunch offerings: pizza, burgers, and an unappealing beef stroganoff.

"Weed makes you everybody's buddy."

No one would argue with that based on his fan club.

We move into the courtyard, and Danny grabs us a bench beneath a shady, inviting tree. After chugging his chocolate milk in a single gulp, he burps. "How's your day going?"

I point at my mouth. "Pretty chill," I say after swallowing.

As soon as I release the last word, I hear the hissing of wheels spinning on uneven ground. I spin around to see a shirtless skateboarder wearing massive Ben Davis jeans with a T-shirt hanging from the back pocket. Bleached blonde hair drapes over his eyes, a tangle of jelly bracelets dangles from his wrist, and a wallet chain swings against his knee.

Time slows. Danny's mouth is still moving, but I barely hear him. I don't want to seem like I have a staring problem, but I can't look away from the skater. He's like a celebrity—his presence here is a middle finger to everything I've learned in my athletic career. As a wrestler, I lifted weights to gain bulk, definition, and tone. It's shocking to see this scrawny guy showing off his underdeveloped physique, rolling through like he owns the school.

But it's more than how he looks; it's the energy he's

giving off. Like the guy enjoys everyone staring and couldn't care less what they think.

The courtyard parts as a line of skaters parade through the lunchtime horde. They all sport sagging pants and lengthy wallet chains, but none match the easy confidence of their leader. Just before reaching the main hall, the commander grips his skateboard and yanks himself into the air. After floating a few inches above the ground, he lands and scoops the board into his arms, breaking into an effortless shuffle.

Some students clap and whoop after his landing. "Nice pressure flip," yells a tan dude in floral shorts. A few jocks snicker, but they're just jealous. This guy has skills, and they know it.

As for me, I can see why they call skate moves "tricks." The main skater kid made that jump look like magic. His followers attempt the same thing but with less success; a tough-looking girl in a brown beanie fares the best.

"Who's that?" I don't need to explain who I mean.

Danny looks up. "Matthias Alexander. You should see him skate at City View." He catches some pizza cheese that falls from his lip. "He's fuckin' rad."

"Fuckin' rad" is an understatement. Matthias is everything I'm not, never have been, and didn't know I wanted to be until this moment. Matthias is a fully formed personality, like a TV character demanding attention, and he's not playing by any rules I know.

"Do you skate?"

"A little," Danny says. "But not like that. Matthias is sick —he should be sponsored."

I've never paid attention to skateboarding apart from watching a couple of video tapes at a friend's birthday party in fourth grade. But when you're a sports obsessive like me, it's easy to recognize when an athlete has something special about them—even one as far away from my expertise as Matthias. "City View," I mutter. "I'll have to check that place out."

The bell rings, and I throw my backpack over my shoulder. I watch Danny hustle off to his next class. He's a nice enough guy, but the only thing I want from him is a pathway to meeting Matthias. Who knew the first day of school would make me so Machiavellian?

FIVE
DUDELINESS

When I show up after school for water polo tryouts, I notice that the locker room is already steamed up and echoing with the screeches of overactive high school boys. I drop my leather Tempe High bag on a bench and get hit in the face by a wave of sensory nostalgia. The combined aromas of Old Spice, Irish Spring, and anti-fungal spray are trapped in the thick air, stinging my eyes.

I've missed this atmosphere: towels whipping, doors slamming, shower heads turning on and off. Locker rooms are always cultural melting pots. Hispanic kids spray their pompadours next to white boys gelling down bangs beside African American dudes using combs to ensure their fades are perfect.

It's all familiar and comfortable, except that every soul here is a stranger to me.

In Tempe, the wrestling team was full of kids I'd known since grade school, like Miguel. On top of that, I was an all-star with lots of wins under my belt. Here, Zack Coleman is nobody, a new face at a new school, trying out for a new sport.

And then there's the Speedo.

Damn, this thing is snug. No way around it—the suit is embarrassing, and this is coming from a guy who used to wear a wrestling onesie. The mirror provides a fogged-up look at my new persona. Six-pack—well, there's an outline of one. Legs look better—some solid muscle from years of mat work. After moving things around in my Speedo, flexing my pecs and biceps, I stride forcefully through the doors to the pool.

Once outside, I see a bunch of boys standing in a semi-circle around a guy with a clipboard. This must be Coach Reardon, who the counselor told me about. He's on the short side with sandy blonde hair and rugged skin. He looks like a coach in an old-fashioned TV sports movie, except he's leaning on a cane. Probably a dramatic college football injury where he got sacked by a hefty linebacker. Or maybe the guy just has a bad knee.

"So," Coach Reardon begins, "the Yellowjackets had a stellar season last year, and I've got no reason to think this one will be any different."

His voice is smooth and controlled, with that hint of ESPN twang all coaches seem to have, no matter where they're from. It's strangely relaxing listening to him talk. Reardon has a presence that makes you feel like he's got everything under control—experience, confidence, or some combination of the two.

"We'll start by swimming a 2400. Then I'll divide all of you up for some scrimmages."

At the last word, a few faces brighten. Evidently, that's what we're here for. "I'll be watching everyone in the water," Reardon continues. "We'll be working on passing, ball handling, and man-down drills."

Good thing I've been brushing up with a water polo basics book. The concept is simple, but like all sports there are endless details. There are seven people in the water at once—six outfield players and a goalie. The most crucial player is called the hole set. They set up with their back to the other team's goal and everyone passes them the ball once offense is in place. I've got no dream of claiming that role; I'm just hoping to hold my own.

I look around at the other guys. We're all sucked into the lilt of Coach Reardon's voice, awaiting further instructions.

"Later, we'll have some general scrimmages to assess gamesmanship." Reardon pauses, reveling in the tension. "OK, get in the pool."

All the guys jump in, and I follow suit, the icy water shocking my system. The over-chlorinated pool, my skintight Speedo hugging my balls, the crisp fall Berkeley morning—it's all unfamiliar.

Guys are bouncing around in the water, warming up. I follow one dude to the wall and start running laps. My form isn't immaculate, and it's tough at first; I can barely get enough air in my lungs. But after a few cycles, I fall into a groove. My wall flips are shaky—some of the polo veterans execute theirs effortlessly—but it could have gone worse.

Finally, Reardon blows his whistle and starts barking names. "Bronski, Davenport, Duffy, Michael, Yang." They splash over to the other side of the pool with the net set up.

"All right, thank you. Coleman, Daniels, Fong, Nielsen."

Maybe it's the cap over my ears, but my last name sounds weird to me. Worse yet, my mind is hammering me with negativity. *What are you doing in a swimming pool? You're a wrestler.* I ignore it all and let momentum kick in, following the other splashing bodies.

The relentless speed of polo is a surprise, and the game is rough as hell. It takes serious attention to keep up and not get dunked, punched, or kicked in the nuts. Once Coach Reardon moves on to the next quartet of guys, the scrimmage plays on repeat in my mind. It wasn't a complete cluster; there was passing, hustling, and I even made one glorious goal.

Back inside, once I've peeled off the Speedo and changed back into street clothes, I realize I'll be heartbroken if I don't make the cut. It's not wrestling, but the feeling of rowdy competition invigorated me.

Outside the locker room, I see a bunch of kids gathered around a piece of yellow paper. Damn, Coach Reardon didn't waste a minute posting his picks.

I inch up to the handwritten list and look for my name. Holy shit—Coleman, Zachary. There it is. Buoyed by triumph, buzzing on adrenaline, I clench my fists. Looks like I'm a Yellowjacket now.

I'm lost in thought when a hand slaps me so hard across my back that I jump. Spinning around, I'm eye to eye with another of the polo guys—Declan Duffy, if I remember the name Coach called correctly. He's wearing Oakley sunglasses with purple lenses that look hella expensive. Like most other guys at tryouts, he looks ripped straight out of *Men's Health*, with broad shoulders and ropey veins across his tanned forearms.

"Hole set again," Declan shouts, draping a meaty arm around my shoulder. His hand is the size of a tennis racket. "Yellowjackets rule!"

I wriggle away and give a half-assed thumbs up. "Stoked to make the team."

"You're new, right?"

"Yeah. From Arizona. I'm Zack."

"Cool, we'll catch up soon," Declan says with a nod that indicates this invitation is compulsory. He then saunters off like the definition of California dudeliness.

It's been a long day. Even though I grew up a staunch atheist, I silently thank God I made the team. Better yet, I didn't end up eating lunch alone on my first day at Berkeley High.

But as cool as it feels to be a Yellowjacket, my mind keeps returning to that wild skater from lunch, and how I want to see more of his world.

SIX

CITY VIEW

"Danny, when's the next time you're going to City View?"

We're in homeroom and I'm trying not to sound too eager, but Danny's so high he doesn't notice. The guy's eyes are as red as a bowl of Hawaiian Punch.

"Everyone just calls it Alameda Skate Park," he says, cluing me in. "Let's hit it up after school. I usually have a few clients hanging around there."

Clients. It never ends with Danny; he's a walking, talking caricature of a pot dealer.

During health education, the teacher takes us to the computer lab where there are stacks of blue and black floppy discs everywhere with magic-markered names like "Anna's Essays" and "GamesGamesGames." Every surface is coated in a thick layer of dust. Summer must have been a slow season up here.

The point of today is for each of us to set up an email account. I choose coletheman@hotmail.com, though I doubt I'll ever use it. Our teacher shows us a video about how to defeat a chain letter, and most kids spend the rest of class playing *The Oregon Trail*. I eventually find some wrestling info when I search on Ask Jeeves. Truthfully, I don't see the point of the internet. I'd rather use the library or read a book or something.

My thoughts keep wandering to the mysterious skatepark known as City View or Alameda or whatever I'm supposed to call it.

After school, Danny shows up in a Corolla that looks like no one's washed it since the '80s. The wheels are so dirt-caked Danny must make deliveries to the backwoods.

"This car reeks of weed," I inform him while buckling my seat belt. "Your parents don't notice?"

"They never use it. But if they did, they wouldn't care." Danny rolls the driver's window down and pats the roof twice. "Shit, I smoke my dad out sometimes."

Getting high with your dad? Berkeley, you're a wacky place for sure.

"Kick back, Zack," Danny says. "Let me you take for a spin around the neighborhood."

As we cruise, Danny blasts nothing but his favorite band, Nirvana. "We're in Oakland now," he explains before launching into a thudding drum roll on the steering wheel. "Berkeley and Oakland are like siblings. But one got all the nice shit, and the other got left to fend for itself."

He's right. Through the soot-streaked passenger window, the city scenery transforms before my eyes. Graffiti-covered buildings, dilapidated cinder-block walls, women in slippers pushing strollers, AC Transit buses exhaling smoke. We're not in college hippie town anymore. My blissed-out driver barely seems to register anything but the music.

"How far is Alameda?"

"Relax," Danny instructs me. "You got somewhere to be?"

"No, I'm good."

Seeing a busted-up payphone on a corner gets my mind whirring. *Uh, Mom, I'm going to be late for dinner. Just driving around with the school pot dealer.*

Danny must sense the tension coming off me because he pats my shoulder. "Dude, we're fine. I'll get you home whenever you need. We're going to take Webster Tube. It goes underwater."

We pass through the tunnel while that big Nirvana radio hit everyone knows blares from his car speakers. I feel like I'm someone else. This whole escapade would never have happened to me back in Tempe.

Soon, Danny pulls into a lot where I see a stone sign that reads: City View Skate Park. He turns the engine off, and the music vanishes.

"This place has concrete bowls, buttery ledges, and flat bars—the whole deal," he informs me. "It used to be a naval base."

"Rad," I reply, wondering what a buttery ledge is.

We step out of the car. Except for a few tufts of early September grass, yellowed and patchy, we've arrived at an industrial wasteland.

"*This* is where Matthias skates?"

"Follow me."

I cram my hands in my pockets and trail Danny as he takes me to a stunning vista.

"Check it, that's the Oakland harbor." Danny says, pointing. "You can even see the SF skyline. Killer view, right?"

"Absolutely."

As promised, Danny guides me straight to the action. A half-dozen skaters glide up and down the sides of the bowl. The sounds of laughing, clapping, coughing, and wheels whizzing on concrete echo across the park. We've reached the promised land.

Danny stands a few feet back from the edge of the bowl

with his arms crossed; I mirror his pose and take in the scene. Skaters are slipping and sliding all over the place. Some land on their knees but quickly receive a hand and are hoisted back onto their boards. Removed from the fast-moving hustle, little kids in helmets and pads ride BMX bikes.

My eyes catch the main event: Matthias, shirtless again, owning every inch of the bowl. No matter how little I know about skateboarding mechanics, it's obvious the dude's form is immaculate. I stand transfixed as he slides smoothly down one side of the bowl and up the other, like a weight on a pendulum, his head peering back over his shoulder, care-free. After gaining momentum, he hoists his lithe body over the top and holds perfectly still, one hand on his board, the other gripping the lip of the bowl. It's dazzling.

As soon as he breaks the pose, a small crowd erupts. "Sick handplant, Matthias," yells a kid in a yellow Carhart jacket.

Everything looks straight out of a movie. Skaters in shirts with blocky logos give each other high fives. Younger kids sit on the sidelines, boards glued to their hands, watching the action but not ready to dive in.

When we read *On the Road* during freshman year, Dad taught me a term that stuck with me: subculture. I've got no desire to ride a skateboard. But this vibe? I want to be a part of it. I'm swept up on a wave of California freedom.

Danny shoves an elbow into my belly. "Matthias is a monster skater, right?"

"Never seen skating like that," I say. "Except on TV or in a movie."

"Exactly." Danny nods to a kid in a beanie with a red flannel tied around his waist.

"This is way cool. Thanks for bringing me." My words come spilling out faster than intended. The energy here is

exhilarating and independent, unlike wrestling matches where everything is reliant on adult rules and whatnot.

"No problem," Danny says. "I'll introduce you to Matthias. He's a client too, sometimes."

Danny strolls along the side of the bowl like a campaigning politician, slapping palms and acknowledging faces with nods along the way. I stick close to him, and soon we reach our destination. Punk music blares from a boombox perched dangerously close to the edge of the bowl.

"Hey, Matthias," Danny says.

The skate hero is sitting on the ground with his head bowed, both hands gripping the top of his board, which he's balancing on its tail. Jutting up like that, the skateboard reminds me of an ancient obelisk I remember seeing in my sixth grade world history textbook.

"Danny Deals," Matthias says, looking up and flipping his bangs back with a lazy twist of his head. "What's up, my man?"

His voice is confident but quieter than I imagined, and it sucks me in. Danny and Matthias perform a complicated handshake that makes my eyes dart back and forth. I'm starting to feel self-conscious in my fitted Gap shorts when Matthias and all the other skaters are swimming in their clothes. Plus, they all have purple streaks, shaved heads, even some mohawks. I discreetly mess up my boring hair.

Danny nudges me forward. "This is my buddy, Zack. He just moved here from Arizona."

Matthias unfolds himself in a single continuous movement until he's standing and offers his hand. For a second, I worry I'm supposed to know their special greeting, but Matthias pulls me into a simple grip.

"Arizona must be so sick," he says. "So, you're like a desert rat. Have you taken peyote?"

In life, there are questions you prepare for. Then there are the ones that catch you entirely off guard—that you look back on for years, rehashing what you could have said instead of what you did. Matthias's question falls in the second bucket.

"I think my dad might have taken it once, or maybe it was acid. I don't know. He left the house for two days wearing only his bathrobe." The words tumble out; talking to Matthias is like being hit with a truth serum.

Danny and Matthias swivel their heads toward each other in unison, like cartoon characters doing a double take.

"His bathrobe?" Matthias spits. "That's dope. I want to hang out with your pops."

Well, that makes two of us.

"Yeah, he's a trip." If Dad's behavior makes me seem intriguing to Matthias, that works for me. I'll take all the help I can get.

They dip into some small talk while I kick my ass internally for being too forthcoming about my screwy family. That's the problem with a truth serum—it wears off, but the revelation sticks around. Kinda like the graffiti on the benches here; you can scrub and paint over the words, but everyone knows it was there. I'll be "Bathrobe Dad Dude" forever.

Matthias grins in my direction. "You like Face to Face?"

I panic. Face to Face? Who is that? "Depends on what song." God, my voice sounds feeble.

He holds up a cracked jewel case with a picture of a barechested guy staring at himself in the mirror. "This whole album shreds."

Before any more lame-ass comments spill from my mouth, Matthias is back in the bowl, performing tricks for a handful of younger kids looking on.

"See that grommet over there?" Danny points at a kid

with a painful-looking sunburn. "That's Matthias's little brother—Noel."

"Grommet?" I've learned that Danny's chill about me asking questions, so I don't feel like a doofus inquiring about the unfamiliar word. The guy's so well-adjusted he makes me think everyone should start smoking weed.

"Grommets are mini-skater kids," Danny explains and then swaggers over to a guy in a Korn shirt and a ball-chain necklace. A deal must be going down.

I look away, not wanting to be complicit, especially with so many youngsters in close proximity.

As it gets darker, the crowd starts to thin. Matthias pulls a T-shirt from his back pocket, slips into it, and flips his skateboard with a kick. He strides over to Danny and me. "You guys should meet us at lunch in the quad tomorrow," Matthias says. "Then we'll head to our dominion, near the bleachers."

"Your dominion," Danny says. "Nice."

Matthias pushes his hair back, and our eyes meet. "See you tomorrow?"

"Definitely. See you then."

"Hell yeah," Matthias says. Then he cups his hand around his mouth and yells, "Noel, time to catch the bus."

Danny drives us back, and we sit silently, listening to the same Nirvana album with the baby on the cover. At one point, when we hit a stoplight, he looks over at me and catches my eye. "Matthias doesn't make a habit of inviting new kids to his zone, Zack. That's serious shit."

I look straight ahead as the light changes. What *does* Matthias see in me? An out-of-towner in ordinary clothes who showed up at his skatepark.

The sun is almost entirely down when Danny drops me off in front of our building. He opens his leather jacket, revealing bulbous inner pockets packed with bags of pot. "You sure you don't need anything?"

"No, man. I'm all good." I step from the car to the curb, tap the roof twice, and start walking. The air is cool, and I feel a pattern of goosebumps rising on my forearms as I cross the courtyard. Fall has a unique mood in California: a sense of change happening, molecules rearranging and forming into new shapes. Everything is in flux—up for grabs.

Our next-door neighbor, Geoff, is pushing open his front door, which reminds me that Mom has office hours right now. It's a fend-for-myself dinner night, but the water polo schedule on the fridge door reminds me to stay disciplined. Pizza rolls are my best bet, so portion control is the name of the game.

Needing a distraction, I sink into the couch with my ten allotted pizza rolls and switch on the TV. Good, *3rd Rock from the Sun* is on. The show is somehow both idiotic and amusing, with this ridiculous premise of aliens on a mission disguised as an American family. But it makes me laugh my ass off, and tonight that does the trick.

For the first time since moving to California, I've legitimately got stuff to look forward to, which is refreshing but stressful. It's weird; playing an entirely new sport feels like no big deal, but the thought of meeting Matthias for lunch is filling me with anxiety.

Against my better judgment, my legs steer me back to the fridge for a few more pizza rolls—screw self-control.

SEVEN
DESERT RAT

I show up in the quad right on time. There is no way I'm blowing my first invite from Matthias by being late. He strides over, skateboard under his arm. I wave my hand at him, then bring it down. Don't want to look as excited as I feel.

Matthias is wearing a white shirt with an A and a tilted crown—the thing is so long on him it looks more like a dress. As for my outfit, I dug out my most worn-out-looking jeans and a pair of Skechers that seem halfway skaterish. This is the best I could do, since none of the crap my mom bought me at the mall is even close to cool.

Following Matthias are a guy and a girl, both scowling and holding skateboards. They remind me of seaweed swaying in the water, lagging a few steps behind their leader.

"Yo, Desert Rat." Matthias drops his board to the ground, crouches low, and rolls directly over to me.

Is that a nickname or something? "Hey, Matthias."

"Follow me, Desert Rat. I'll take you to where we kick it." Matthias's words flow out in a breathy stream.

"No doubt," I say, immediately feeling dumb.

I can feel eyes checking us out as we wade through the ocean of students. Their attention makes me hyper-aware of my distinct lack of a skateboard. Can you be part of this pack and not skate?

"Rob, you bring a lighter?" Matthias asks a dark-haired guy with acne on his neck and a big butt accentuated by too-tight jeans.

"You know it." Rob's wearing a dark blue shirt with a busty cartoon girl and HOOK-UPS across the front. All these kids have crazy shirts. My snug, plain beige one is not cutting it.

Matthias leads us across the football field and behind the bleachers until we arrive at a concrete strip bordered by a wooded area. Cigarette butts and skid marks on the ground indicate that skating happens here. This must be their dominion.

Matthias lets his board slip from his arm to the ground and executes a quick kick-flip.

I sit down and pull out my tuna sandwich and Ruffles. Eat, but don't get too full. Gotta be strict for polo.

Matthias rolls over to me. "Desert Rat, you're tight with Danny." He stops in front of me and mimes hitting a joint. "You got some weed?"

I place my hands behind each bicep, pushing them out like Bret Hart does in photos. "I made the water polo team, so I'm not smoking."

He pulls his shirt off and stuffs it in his back pocket as usual, so it hangs like a tail. "You swim? Rad."

I look away from Matthias's bare torso. "Well, wrestling is my real sport, but people say our team is pretty weak."

"True that."

"So, my counselor convinced me to try out for polo." The word counselor rings in my ears, sounding very lame.

No matter, Matthias is already skating off. Even with headphones covering both his ears, the sounds of sharp guitars and barked vocals escape. Soon, he's spinning in a circle, lost in his own world.

Tina is wearing a blue Santa Cruz sweatshirt and brown Dickies pants. Strands of hair poke out the back of her beanie like wheat. She yells, "Matthias!"

He waits a few seconds before pulling his headphones down and letting them dangle around his neck.

"Can you believe how boring math was today?" Tina asks, happy to have his attention.

"Dude," he replies, stretching the word into two syllables, "I wasn't awake enough to be bored." Without warning, Matthias kicks his board away and starts flinging himself around, grunting along to the music.

"Watch this pressure flip," Rob shouts at the others and stomps on the back of his skateboard clumsily as he slides one Vans-clad foot in the other direction. The jump was nothing to write home about, but Rob wears a satisfied smile.

"Rob," Tina says, "you need to slide your front foot up the nose more." She rolls a few feet, crouches, leaps up, slams the back of her board, and jumps into the air. "Now, *that's* a pressure flip for you," Tina says after a smooth landing, her jump easily twice the height of Rob's. He looks dejected and impressed at the same time.

I take in the skate show from my seat while munching on my chips and sandwich. With their random movements, the trio reminds me of those bumbling Pac-Man ghosts. Rob is throwing moves to impress Tina while she's working to capture the attention of Matthias, who is dancing by himself in a distracted circle, letting his skateboard drift across the concrete.

Rob joins me and lowers himself onto his board, where

he rocks lazily from side to side. It's easy to feel bad for this guy, a loner even among friends. "Want a Ruffle?" I ask.

He shakes his head and pulls a PowerBar from his pocket; the golden wrapper is torn open, revealing a half-eaten beige blob with tooth marks.

"Need to drop some weight." Rob rips off a chunk with the side of his mouth. "I bring a couple of these every day," he says, jaw moving with great effort.

"I get it. In Tempe, we had to weigh in for wrestling matches. The whole team was always dropping and gaining pounds."

Out of nowhere, Matthias appears, his face streaked with sweat. He grips my shoulder and lifts me from my seat. "Good hang. Right, Desert Rat?"

If anyone else at Berkeley High, or anywhere, called me Desert Rat, it would be instant mortification, self-esteem splattered all over the bleachers. But Matthias isn't mocking me. It's like he's giving me a boost to fit in better with his gang.

"What were you listening to?"

"'Time Bomb' by Rancid from ...*And Out Come the Wolves*." Matthias wiggles back into his shirt. "Best East Bay punk band ever. If you like them, you should check out Gilman. I'll take you."

"That would be rad," I say to Matthias's back as he rolls away.

"New guy probably doesn't even know what Gilman is," Rob says through a mouthful of PowerBar.

He's correct, of course.

Tina glares at Rob from beneath her beanie. "Gilman is an all-ages punk club," she tells me. "Unfortunately, my uptight churchy family thinks the place is satanic and won't let me go."

"That sucks," I say. Thank God for my atheist parents.

In the distance, the bell rings, and we start walking back to campus. Directly in front of me, I see Rob mouth, "That would be rad," to Tina, mocking my ignorance about Gilman, skating, and everything else.

Rob pisses me off, but I feel like Matthias is above his childish shit. For some reason, I'm starting to think we have a connection, like ESP, something Matthias doesn't share with these junior skaters who idolize him.

Still, there will always be the Robs of the world trying to throw me off my game, so I have to beware of ticking time bombs and wolves coming out.

EIGHT
LIKE ROYALTY

For the rest of the week, as I navigate from class to class to polo practice, the question of cliques invades my thoughts. Who will my allies be at Berkeley High—the jocks or the skaters? Even though Matthias is light years more intelligent than the kids I met at tryouts, I'm now a Yellowjacket, a jock, a water polo bro. Can someone live on both sides of the divide?

Case in point. After seventh period on Thursday, Declan from the polo team corners me at my locker.

"Nice setup yesterday," he says. "Want to head off campus and get burgers with me and the crew?"

Here's the deal. Newbie players like me get grandfathered into the popularity system, which means everyone expects you to hang out with your teammates. The problem is I told Matthias I'd come to their afternoon skate session today. For reasons I can't fully explain, I'd rather be behind the bleachers with the skaters than making uncomfortable small talk with meatheads.

"Man, I'm sorry, but I promised some friends I'd hang

with them." The entire skate posse appears on cue, moving like a multi-armed cephalopod.

Declan points with his thumb. "Those people?"

"Yeah, guess I should hit it."

"Do your thing," he says with a shrug, joining up with a gang of waiting polo players.

Happily off the hook, I bounce over to Matthias, feeling like one of those tiny iron fillings getting pulled to a magnet.

"Greetings, Dr. Z."

"Dr. what?"

"That's the new name I'm bestowing upon you." Matthias lifts his skateboard and gives my head a light tap, like he's anointing me.

"And how'd I earn this honor?"

"Glad you asked that good sir," Matthias says. "The 'd' and 'r' are from Desert Rat. Plus, you're smart. Danny said your mom's a professor."

It sounds suspiciously like people have been talking about me, which doesn't do much for my new kid paranoia. Let's test whether the nickname game goes both ways. "OK, if I'm Dr. Z, then you're Matty."

My new friend takes a moment to consider the suggestion before saying, "Matty it is." He then does a half-bow and twirls his hand like he's unfurling a giant scroll. "After you, Dr. Z."

"Why, thank you, Matty." Somehow, we're both doing these fake Shakespearean accents, and it feels chill—as if the two of us made an unspoken decision to act dorky.

We caravan to the skater dominion, and I do feel like royalty, like second in command to a high-ranking officer. As far as I know, Matthias doesn't have unique monikers for Tina or Rob, another clue that we share a deeper bond.

"Dr. Z, do you go on the internet?"

"Yeah, they made us sign up for Hotmail in the computer lab."

"You need to check out Ultimate Band List, dude," Matthias says. "It's a gold mine of musical information."

Leave it to Matthias to find the coolest thing on the World Wide Web. "What's your email address? Mine's coletheman@hotmail.com."

"Me? I'm barkingtrucks21@hotmail.com," he says with a glint in his eye.

"Sick."

It's an overcast afternoon, and the crew seems spacey and tired by the time we reach their area. But not Matthias; he's spinning everywhere, extending his limbs like a Wacky Wall Walker toy. I immediately see this as less a session than a demonstration featuring one skater. Rob and Tina aren't trying any tricks, just watching from beneath the bleachers, clapping for Matthias's moves as noisy punk rock blares from his headphones.

Rob takes a swig from a Diet Dr. Pepper bottle. "Zack, what do you *usually* do after school when you're not slumming with the skate rats?"

"Practice and homework, I guess."

He rips off a chunk of PowerBar, mashes it up in his hands until it's a small ball, then pops it in his mouth. "Dude, you're such a preppy."

"Guess so, Rob." I'm not going to let his needling bug me today. I've got Rob figured out—he worships Matthias and is infatuated with Tina. On top of that, the guy is fully awkward on his skateboard.

Rob looks over at Tina. "Don't you think the new guy should be with his polo brothers?"

"Shouldn't you start eating real food?" Tina asks. "If I watch you consume one more energy bar, you'll be cleaning up my puke."

Matthias ducks beneath the bleachers, hanging those lanky arms from the metal beams. With a swing of his head, he faces Rob. "Chill, dude. Zack's no regular jock. Dr. Z has a desert soul."

My new buddy to the rescue. Matthias acts like he's not engaged, but in reality, he seems to hear every word his followers say.

"Want some real food, Rob?" I offer the bagel I didn't eat at lunch. No point holding onto hard feelings, especially since Matthias told him to back off.

Rob stares at the bagel in my hand like it's a sirloin steak. "Screw it," he says. "I'm starving. Thanks, Dr. Z."

"It's Zack." Only one person here gets to call me by my new nickname—and it sure as shit isn't Rob.

"Whatever." Rob claws through the wax sandwich paper until he's got cream cheese all over his hands and face like a kindergartner. Against my better judgment, I find it endearing.

Matthias tosses his backpack over his shoulder and reaches for his board. The others acknowledge the signal and immediately start packing up their things. I guess the skate sesh is over.

"Dr. Z, let's hit Telegraph on Saturday. You down?"

"Saturday? That works," I say, trying to conceal my excitement. Out of the corner of my eye, I see Rob perk up.

Matty parades in front of us, brandishing his board like a machete. "Cool. Meet me at People's Park at noon, and we'll see what transpires on the Ave."

Transpires. Excellent vocab choice—Dad would be impressed. Matthias has a language all his own.

"So, what exactly do you mean by me having a desert soul?"

"Not sure, Dr. Z. Something tells me you comprehend things most people don't."

Matthias stops, grabs both my shoulders, and looks into my eyes through a falling curtain of hair. "It's a good thing, my desert dude," he says. "We're the same, you and me. I've never even left Cali, but I have a traveler's spirit. You may not be a skater, but you know about being in the flow, catching the moment."

I'm trapped in the pull of the Matthias tractor beam.

"You just need some fuckin' punk rock education. That's all," he says.

"I'm ready for it."

"I know, Dr. Z. That was obvious the minute we met."

And with that, I watch as my self-appointed punk instructor loiters off, his pants sliding off his butt and across the dirty ground. The halls are nearly empty now, just me and a handful of students still around after school.

As I walk home, my brain is bubbling with new nicknames, new destinations, and a new companion. But one question hovers above the chaos. What exactly did Matthias mean by punk rock education?

NINE
MOTHER-SON TIME

Beep…Beep…Beep…

I smash the alarm and sit up straight in bed as my mom thumps on my door.

"Wake up, kiddo."

"I'm awake." It's Saturday morning, and now that I'm up, my mind begins bouncing in every direction. But all thoughts lead to the same place: Today, I'm hanging out with Matthias on Telegraph Avenue.

"Mom, can I get a ride to Telegraph to meet my friend, Matthias?"

"A friend?" She sounds overjoyed. "Telegraph meets right up with campus. I'll drop you off and get some work done at the lab."

No fucking chance. Mom in loose hippie attire talking to my slouching skater pal? That does not compute. "How about you drive me to Cal, show me around, then I hook up with Matthias?"

"That's an acceptable plan," she says. "So it's *Cal* now. Looks like someone's starting to learn the local vernacular."

"Jesus, Mom. Why do you have to get so involved in my life?"

"Who's involved?" she says, taking a sip of coffee. "Can't a mother be pleased that things are working out for her son?"

"I made a friend. Let's not get carried away."

To get a ride, I've got to visit my mom's work and let her take me on the grand tour. Screw it. No pain, no gain.

On the drive, Mom talks about her department while I consider how much I prefer the Bay Area climate to Arizona's. You want a light blue sky with coloring book clouds? Check. Rolling hills? They're in ample supply. Berkeley is the shit when it comes to weather, even if it takes until the afternoon for the marine layer to burn off most days.

"Here we are," Mom says.

We leave the car in faculty parking and set off on foot. As we walk, Mom reaches both arms up to the sky and shakes them like she's doing some ancient ceremonial dance. Luckily, there aren't many people on campus at this hour on a Saturday.

"Can you believe all these redwoods and pine trees?"

"Yup, trees are cool."

"Zack, would it kill you to at least act like you're impressed?" She points at a bell tower with clocks on all sides jutting into the blue sky. "That's Sather Tower, but everyone calls it the Campa*nile*." She hits the third syllable hard.

"Campanile," I repeat.

Mom walks ahead of me and keeps talking tour-guide style. "It's named after an Italian landmark."

I have to admit, UC Berkeley is what colleges look like in the movies—dramatic and inspiring, a place you want to be. I wonder if I could ever get into this school. Good thing I don't have to worry about that for a couple of years.

We end up at the Greek Theater, which is an amphitheater with a row of columns behind the stage. We can't see inside, but there are photos around the box office.

"Jerry Garcia and the Grateful Dead played here often," Mom declares like she's reciting a piece of US history.

"Tight," I say, though I doubt either of us can name a single Grateful Dead song.

Finally, after huffing across a few manicured lawns, we arrive at an old-fashioned brick building with a red roof. The marble plaque near the doors reads College of Letters and Science. "And this," Mom says, hand on hip, "is where your mother works."

She leads me inside and gives me a quick walk-through of her department, stopping to greet a few colleagues putting in weekend hours. Mom is in her happy place, and it's obvious how much her peers respect her.

When we get to her office, she runs a hand under a gold plate with her name on it. "Welcome to my digs."

"Dang, Mom, you've gone pro. This is like nationals for professors." The room's twice as spacious as her ASU office, and she's decked it out with degrees, awards, and a few framed posters from our Tempe house, where we had more room to decorate.

I walk over to her desk and pick up a framed photo taken on Halloween when I must have been nine or ten. I'm peeking out from behind Dad in a stupid-ass Power Rangers costume. He's dressed up as the poet Walt Whitman, which wasn't that much of a stretch; he just wore a peacoat and put white powder all over his bushy beard.

"Remember how Dad used to read the works of people like Kurt Vonnegut and Anne Sexton out loud instead of letting me watch action movies?"

Mom laughs. "Yes, your father has very specific taste in literature, art, and films."

"He did sit through the entire *Die Hard* series with me."

"Is that true?" She lowers her glasses.

"Yup, he called them 'intellectually vacuous, but harmless.'"

"That sounds like Silas."

"I have to admit, I was surprised to see a picture with Dad on your desk," I say, putting the photo back where I found it.

"A reminder of better times. Plus, you look so cute, I couldn't help it."

It's true. We both look happy, and Dad's even smiling for once.

Mom taps her desk with a pen. "Anyway, let's get a bite before you meet your friend. There are a ton of places to eat on campus."

We end up at a small taqueria that smells of salt and lime. The decor consists of a few giant straw sombreros on the walls. Our waiter brings us a mountain of chips before we even crack a menu—a place after my own hungry heart.

"So, tell me about school. Are there any significant differences between here and Tempe?"

"Whoa, that's a huge question. How about an easier one?"

"OK, have you made any new friends aside from this Matthias?"

"There's one guy named Danny Chang who seems cool." No need to mention that he is also the school's foremost weed dealer.

Mom claps her hands together and an old guy next to us looks up from his messy page of equations. "A nice Asian boy," she says. "It's great you're meeting people from so many different backgrounds here."

"Mom, that's totally racially insensitive. I knew tons of Asian kids back home. Plus, Tempe High was majority Hispanic."

"Of course, you're right." She concentrates on her enchilada. "And what about girls?"

Outside the window, a group of students run across a field in pursuit of a Frisbee. I watch them for a few moments before answering. "Yes, there are girls."

"You must hate talking about this sort of thing with me."

"It's not my absolute favorite subject in the world." While this is true, my reluctance is more because there isn't anything of substance to share.

"Fair enough. When you're ready, you know I'm here."

"It's weird being in a new city without Dad—almost feels like we're running away."

She clinks her knife down on her plate. "We're not the ones running, Zack."

"So many of my friends have parents who split up, but they see the other one every other weekend."

"I know you want to see your father. I'd like that for you too. But that isn't the space he's in. I wish things were different, but here we are."

"Here we are."

Mom looks like she might cry. I hate this whole conversation, hate all the shitty emotions it dredges up, hate that we've had it so many times over the past two years.

She crosses her arms. "His episodes, his outbursts. We needed some healthy distance—*I* needed some healthy distance."

"Right."

"Your father is a brilliant, kind, artistic man."

"Brilliant but bonkers."

"That's an inelegant word. Let's not use it."

"Don't forget when he left our house in his bathrobe and

didn't come home for two days." The statement hangs there like the smell of sulfur.

"I remember, Zack. That doesn't make a person bonkers. Your father has his battles, like we all do," she says. "You know how hard we tried to make things work, but this is how it ended up. I've made peace with it."

"*You* tried to make things work," I say. "Dad just floated away, stopped teaching, and started waking up in the afternoon after staying up all night working on his poems."

"You're right. Silas's instability drove a wedge between us."

I flash to waking up in the middle of a scorching July night: Dad in the living room wearing nothing but his underwear, sweat all over his face, plunking away at his typewriter.

Mom pats my arm. "I understand you miss having your father around to throw a football with and do dad things."

I laugh. "We never threw a football. Dad lectured me about Allen Ginsberg and Maya Angelou."

Right now, two sides of my personality are duking it out. "Understanding Zack" gets that divorce is part of life and happens to countless families. "Bratty Zack" wants his father around and doesn't give two shits about courts and custody agreements. "Don't you wonder what he's doing now?"

Mom reaches across the table and takes my hands in hers. They're cold but feel good. I try to look tough like The Ultimate Warrior or Kane, but it doesn't work on someone who's seen you wet your bed.

"Whatever he's doing probably involves copious amounts of tequila and not enough showering." She rises and lifts her purse. "Forget I said that. That wasn't good parental behavior."

"Nah, it's cool when you're honest with me."

"C'mon, I'll show you the Rec Facility. There's a colossal gym, and faculty families can use it for free."

That's my mother for you. She knows nothing will improve my mood faster than a chance to lift weights. Still, there are more important matters at hand. "Thanks, but I've gotta go meet Matthias."

Telegraph Avenue beckons.

TEN

DIRTY HANDS

As I cross UC Berkeley en route to Telegraph, the world looks incredibly vivid, from the still-green grass to the turning leaves, which are a novelty to me. But then I see Matthias at the park entrance, and the pleasant feeling downshifts, heads straight to my guts, and morphs into a violent, rumbling belly.

He's practicing what looks like a wheelie on the nose of his board, instead of the tail. As usual, the Discman is turned up so loud you can hear it from nearly an entire city block away.

"Hey, Matty."

He pops his head up and skates over. "You made it," Matty says. "This your first time on the Ave?"

"Not my first. I think my mom took me to a bookstore near here."

"Well, today will be a whole other level," he says. "Dr. Z and Matty are gonna take Telegraph by storm."

Matthias smiles wide, and I notice that one of his front teeth is a nasty shade of yellow. Didn't Matthias's parents make him go to the dentist? My preteen years were a hellscape of braces and all those torturous tightening sessions, but at least now my mouth looks decent. Maybe Matty is above the basic rules of dental hygiene.

"So, what's Rob up to today?"

Matthias lets his headphones fall around his neck. "Rob from school? No idea."

"Thought you guys were all tight. You, Tina, everyone."

Matthias draws some phlegm up and spits on the grass. "Tina's becoming a good skater," he says. "Rob is whatever. There will always be followers like that, man."

This meager assessment of Rob is a thrilling revelation but not a good enough reason for me to break my cool.

People's Park is all around us—open lawns peppered with palm trees and hand-painted signs that could have been around in the '60s. As we pass some overflowing garbage cans that make me gag, Matthias elbows me in the ribs and points at some disheveled kids not much older than us.

"I know these gutter punks." In a series of seamless movements, he drops his board, hops on it, and skates over to them. "Yo, Anthony."

A boy with patches all over his black jeans, holding a chain connected to a scarred-up pit bull, turns his head in slow motion. "Ma...tthi...as," he croaks.

"What's going down?" Matthias slaps the guy's hand and pulls him in for an embrace.

God knows what Anthony smells like. With the accumulation of black filth on his neck, it looks like he's slept under a bench or in someone's backyard. It seems sensible to keep my distance. Thankfully, Matthias doesn't linger too long.

"Sorry to keep you waiting, man," he says as we fall back into formation. "Hadn't talked to that dude in a while."

"No problem."

"There's a whole scene down here," Matthias says,

giving a seminar to a class of one. "Crusties, traveler kids, punk nomads—whatever you want to call them. They hop trains, move from town to town. Denver, New Orleans, Portland. It's a subculture."

There's that word again. "Like in *On the Road*."

"Yeah, man," Matthias says. "They live on the road."

"No, like the Jack Kerouac book. The Beat poets."

"Exactly."

That's all Matthias says, so he obviously doesn't know about Kerouac. Thanks, Dad. You may be a flake who wants to avoid contact with your family, but you taught me about the Beat Generation, among other things.

Matthias skates ahead, ducking his head beneath a tree branch. He's showing off, and it's a blast just watching him cut loose on the street.

Soon, we're in the heart of Telegraph, and Matthias was right, the Avenue is alive. Incense clouds waft out of storefronts covered in psychedelic artwork, mingling with the smells of kebabs and pizza. Tourists, students, hippies, yuppies—everyone is bumping into each other in a chaotic rush.

Matthias is in his element, giving me insider details about everything. He motions to a used clothing place with a row of mannequins in the window, all wearing trendy clothes. One's even sporting baggy jeans and skate shoes.

"That's Buffalo Exchange," Matthias explains. "It's decent, but it's better to hit up Goodwill if you want to score the sick threads."

"Buffalo Exchange started in Arizona," I say. But I catch his drift; my mall clothes are not up to par.

"Now, I'm gonna introduce you to the best pizza in the Bay Area."

Matthias takes us to a place called Slice of Life. Of course, he knows the cashier, a senior from our school with stringy, dirty-blonde hair wearing a heavy metal T-shirt with an illegible band name. The guy gives us four slices for the price of a fountain soda.

"I have to charge something to put it in the system," he apologizes. "But no one counts the pizza at the end of the day."

My two pieces of pepperoni are not only the best pizza I've tasted in the Bay Area—they're the most delicious of my sixteen-year existence. No question. Matthias has Telegraph Avenue under his thumb. My tour guide reveals our final stop after we roll ourselves out of Slice of Life in a food coma.

"One last spot to take you to," Matthias says, smiling with a piece of cheese dangling from his mouth. "A magical place where the music runs free, and you can find anything you want to hear."

"A CD store?"

Matthias shakes his head in mock disappointment. "Where I'm taking you is more than a mere CD store," he says. "We're going to Amoeba."

A few blocks later, we come upon a glass building with rock posters all over the windows. I've been to record shops; this looks like a castle of music.

Inside the front door, there's a guy on a stool in a hat that says Pennywise reading an issue of *Alternative Press*. "You have to check your jackets and that skateboard," he tells us.

We hand over the goods, and the doorman passes each of us a clothespin. "Enjoy Amoeba," he says, returning to his magazine.

This place is serious. There are rows of CDs, tapes, and records everywhere I look. There's also an impressive DVD section where I bet there are some rad wrestling movies, but I'm not ready to reveal that side of myself to Matthias.

All the employees have dyed hair and piercings, like

Matthias, but way more extreme. I see shirts with names I don't recognize, like Daniel Johnston and Drive Like Jehu. The guys all have greasy hair hanging in their faces, and the girls look like they could melt you on the spot through their librarian glasses.

Matthias notices me staring. "Hipsters," he says. "They know everything about music."

"They're intimidating," I say, "but in a nerdy way."

"They like to act superior." Matthias heads over to the Used New Arrivals aisle. "No way," he says, enthralled by the back of a CD. "I've been looking for this Operation Ivy record forever."

"Operation who?"

"It's some of the dudes from Rancid when they were a ska band." He's on a quest, moving down the aisle, thumbing through CDs without looking up.

"I've never heard of most of these bands," I say. "Wait, I know The Offspring."

"Dude, if you like them, check out Bad Religion." Matthias shows me a CD with five moody-looking guys and the words *Stranger Than Fiction* on the cover. "Greg Griffin's lyrics will change your entire global outlook. He's a punk professor."

Then, like it's the most normal thing in the world, Matthias slips the Bad Religion CD into the front of his pants—between his Joe Boxers and his belly. With his billowing T-shirt providing cover, he silently pulls off the plastic sensor strip and sticks it to the side of the bin. Two seconds later, Matthias is looking at CDs like nothing happened.

What. The. Fuck?

My vision blurs as I stand motionless in the aisle, and the moldy vinyl smell threatens to make me pass out—time to start moving.

I fake-browse and take stock of the situation. Rambling thoughts pop around my brain, latching onto each other and growing into random shapes, like the splat behind the store name on the neon sign outside.

"So, what bands are you into?" my criminal friend asks me.

There's no way in hell I'm admitting the last album I bought was the *Men in Black* soundtrack. Plus, I'm distracted knowing Matthias has a CD pressed against his body. Even worse, I think he intends to leave without paying for it.

"I like Goo Goo Dolls and Eminem," I reply, trying to come up with a half-cool answer.

"We'll ween you off that mainstream garbage, Dr. Z. Just wait."

A minute passes, and no one handcuffs us. I'm breathing easier as I follow Matthias to the hip-hop section.

"We all need someone to direct us to the delicacies, like this album." He holds up *Beats, Rhymes and Life* by A Tribe Called Quest. Matthias peels the sticker off, puts the CD in his waistband behind Bad Religion, and lets his shirt drop.

I turn away, but Matthias keeps talking and browsing. "Oh, nice. Wu-Tang Clan. I'm buying this right now."

He's buying and stealing from the same place—at the same time?

"I'm going to check out the posters." Without releasing my breath, I cross the store and start flipping through the plastic frames, trying to act casual while every cell screams, "Get the hell out of here."

After a few minutes, a hand taps me on my shoulder.

"You find anything?" Matthias asks.

I pull out a random tube with Beastie Boys on the label. "This one."

"Beastie Boys, nice. *Ill Communication* is a killer album. Let's bounce." We stroll up to the front counter, where a guy with two eyebrow rings awaits us with a gloomy look. Matthias places Operation Ivy and Wu-Tang Clan on the counter.

"$25.98," Eyebrow Ring says, sounding like a robot.

"No sweat." Matthias yanks his wallet from his back pocket, and the lengthy dog chain clanks against the counter. He removes two twenties, slides them to the cashier, and winks at me.

"$14.02 is your change. Have a nice day."

Matty hangs beside me as I buy my Beastie Boys poster.

My heart feels like it's thumping louder than the music. We passed one test, but we're not in the clear yet. I walk through the security machine first, my breath trapped between my lungs and lips. Once I'm on the other side, I return the clothespin, my index finger flattened where I've been using it to cut off my blood flow. The doorman retrieves my jacket from a cubby, and I enter the bright outside world of freedom. What just happened?

Matthias exits a few seconds later, bag in one hand, skateboard in the other. We walk a block in silence before he draws both CDs out of his underwear and hands them to me. "There you go—hip-hop and punk rock lesson numero uno."

We spend the rest of the afternoon messing around on Telegraph. I even take a brief spin on Matthias's skateboard as a joke. I've got decent balance from wrestling, so I make it a whole city block. I kick the deck when I disembark, imitating how I've watched Matthias do it.

"Not bad, Dr. Z. Not bad at all."

Like I said, I pick up athletic stuff fast.

And it turns out Anthony the gutter punk isn't the only character Matthias knows. Every few feet, we run into a grommet, a punk, and even normal kids from school, all falling over themselves to praise Matthias for his skating.

He's a star, and with my build, I feel like a personal body-guard, someone cool and important.

It's going great until I see a street clock. "I'm supposed to meet my mom back on campus at three."

"Or what, you turn into a pumpkin?"

"No, it's just—"

"I'm joking, Dr. Z."

Matthias pulls me in for a hug and I stiffen. I guess I'm not used to that kind of contact outside of sports.

"Do your thing," he says. "But make sure to listen to both those CDs tonight. That's your homework."

"You know I will. See you at lunch on Monday."

On my jog back, I pass the same funky boutiques and eateries, the bag with my poster and contraband whacking my side in rhythm with my breath. I'm no longer worried about the CD heist or the awkward hug. That unfamiliar contentment from this morning is back. I feel alive.

I make it to Mom's office a few minutes late, sweaty and breathless. She looks me up and down and points at my bag. "What did you buy, kiddo?"

Does she have a sixth sense? "Couple of CDs and a poster for my room."

"Anyone I've heard of?"

"Bad Religion and A Tribe Called Quest." I take a seat. "So, no, you haven't heard of them."

Mom looks like she swallowed a lemon rind. "Bad Religion?"

———

Once we get home, I rush to my room, climb on the bed, and rip a poster of a wrestler named Razor Ramon off the wall, replacing him with Beastie Boys. I stand back to gauge the effect. Much better.

Next, I kick off my shoes and sit on the floor. Using my house key, I remove the plastic from both CD cases and spread them out in front of me. On one side is the drab blueish-gray Bad Religion cover. On the other is A Tribe Called Quest, which is all brightly colored images of a burning clock tower, buildings, and a basketball court in a bombed-out city. In the foreground is a red and green super-hero holding a flag with the group's name.

This is a world I've never experienced but instantly want to visit: a magical graffiti comic book come to life. I drop the CD in, press play, and listen to the machine whir as I wait for the first song to start.

Dust, crackle, an ancient electric piano.

A funky beat kicks in.

I lie on my back in the middle of the floor and let the chorus of voices transport me. Fifty-one minutes later, I awaken from my trance. Matthias was right. I needed some guidance. I've been listening to the equivalent of McDonald's, while this music is gourmet food for my soul.

I start the album over from the beginning.

Since the divorce, it's felt like things have been out of my control. Like I'm being led around by Mom, coaches, whoever. Something changed when Matthias pulled those CDs from his waistband and placed them in my hand. Suddenly, I was no longer a bystander. Now, I'm in his world, his scene.

As the quirky, brainy hip-hop of A Tribe Called Quest saturates the air, I feel empowered. I run my fingers over the smooth CD cover and play the day back in my mind. I must admit, it felt good to get my hands dirty for a change.

ELEVEN
OFF THE RAILS

When I hit the water this morning, the pool feels positively frigid, but I grit my teeth and fall into our drills—backstroke partner passing, submerge and flip, and the brutal ten-minute eggbeater. Who knew treading water could hurt that much? Water polo may be childish compared to Matthias's world of punk rock and petty theft, but this is my new sport, and I'm in it to win it.

In the middle of our first scrimmage, Declan elbows me hard in the ribs and steals the ball. The taste of over-chlorinated water fills my mouth as I go under. For a moment, there's a fleeting desire to surrender, to say "screw it." But I force myself to start treading water, then race to retrieve what's rightfully mine.

I smack my hand down on the yellow rubber ball and grab it away, water splashing in every direction. "No regrets," I yell directly into Declan's ear. That's one of Coach Reardon's favorite sayings. It means leaving it all in the pool. We're here to dominate, and nothing but our best is good enough.

Once I've taken possession, Declan seems lost in a daze.

He isn't playing hole set during this scrimmage so he's off his game. I pass to this guy Stevie for an easy goal.

Reardon pounds his cane against the ground a few times in a row. "Nicely done, Coleman."

Point made. For the rest of practice, I lay back and let other players take control. Reardon blows the whistle, and we rush like lemmings to the wall to exit the pool. After shaking some water from my ear, I hock up a loogie and spit at the ground. My ribs ache where Declan got me.

The steamed-up locker room offers some relief from the morning chill, and as I towel off, I take in the post-game chatter like it's background music. I'm not comfortable enough with the other players to interject comments, but I laugh along.

Declan slams his locker shut. "Coleman, you seem pretty tight with Captain Cuckoo."

I zip my jeans up and face my accuser. "Who?"

"Captain Cuckoo, Matthias Alexander." Declan's back is against his locker now, backpack slung over one shoulder. That big guy Nelson from my homeroom flanks him, snickering like he's on *Beavis and Butthead*.

"We hang out sometimes." I pull my shirt over my head. "He's a cool guy." Out of the corner of my eye, I see some other players slip out of the locker room.

"I've known that dude since we were kids." Declan gestures to Nelson. "Lot of us have. Matthias went crazy in sixth grade."

Here's the second sneak attack of the day. He steps right up to me and pulls an invisible piece of lint off my shirt. "We thought you should know, being new and all."

"I don't know what the hell you're even talking about." I hear myself, but I'm getting the same feeling as in Amoeba when Matthias snagged those CDs. Apprehension. Adrenaline. Anger. All at once.

Despite Declan being a generic jock, I thought he was a decent person. I was dead wrong. Now, I want to put him in a camel clutch, and I could. He has no fucking clue what I'm capable of, doesn't even know I used to wrestle.

Nelson giggles. "Tell him, D."

"Your friend freakin' lost it," Declan says. "Started smashing his face against the cafeteria table, yelling about how he wasn't from Earth. Kids were losing their minds—crying and calling for their mommies. Matthias Alexander spent most of that year in the psych ward."

I keep my face entirely still. No expression. Like a wrestler before a match.

Declan gives me a shit-eating grin. "They gave him a ton of drugs in there. He was different when he came back, kinda out of it."

"That's when he went skater," Nelson adds.

I turn away from the two of them, click my Master Lock, and give the numbers a spin. "Appreciate the warning, Declan."

"What's it like hanging out with that guy?"

"Matthias? Well, he's a musical encyclopedia, not to mention a mind-blowing skater."

"Because he rolls around school?" Nelson asks.

I shake my head. "No, he's like pro level. He could make skating a career."

Declan laughs. "What, he's like Tony Hawk or something? I've never seen him do anything that impressive."

"You need to see him at City View." I'm desperate for this exchange to end, get back to my real life, and sort out what's true from what's locker-room crap.

"We thought you should know the real deal. Yellow-jackets look after each other."

Bullshit. "Thanks for sharing."

Blood pumping in my ears, I leave the locker room

without looking back. Outside, the morning fog feels oppressive, and I take the long way to homeroom for a few minutes to think.

For the next few hours, everything is a blur. Thanks to Declan, I keep flashing to a creepy image of Matthias getting pulled from class in a straitjacket. The whole situation has me hella stressed out.

Then, midway through fourth period, the truth slams me like a piledriver by The Undertaker. That was Declan's retaliation for me working him over in practice. He's forcing me to pick sides, whereas the old me was content to drift along, friends with everyone but tight with no one. Declan poisoned my mind, and I've got to get the real story.

At lunch, I meet Matty, Rob, and Tina in the usual spot. Matty's headphones are blasting at maximum volume, and I hear a voice yodeling something about a holiday in Cambodia. The three of them are discussing a video of Tony Hawk at the X-Games.

Tina shakes her head. "Sickest vert runs I've ever seen."

"Yeah, but what about the 900 that took him ten times to make?" Rob looks back and forth between Matty and Tina for affirmation.

Tina pantomimes the move with her hand. "He kept pushing himself even though it was past regulation time. Hawk's got heart."

Rob's so overjoyed by her attention it's nauseating. "How many ribs do you think that fool's broken?" He keeps his back to me as he talks, which I'm learning not to take personally.

I remember Declan's condescending comment about Matthias being like Tony Hawk, probably the only pro skater name he could conjure. Not that I know many more, but I've heard Rob and Tina praise Danny Way, Mark Gonzales, Elissa Steamer, and a bunch of others.

Matthias brings the volume down on his Discman and sits beside me. "You look stressed, my brother."

I hoped I could do this when it was just us. Screw it. "I heard some messed-up things about you this morning, dude."

"Enlighten me," Matty says while spinning one of his skateboard's scuffed, dusty wheels. He's trying to sound casual, but I can tell he's interested, even worried.

"Some polo guys said you went off the rails in sixth grade."

Tina pulls her beanie over her eyes and does a dramatic backward fall.

Matty lets out a forced laugh. "Let me guess. Declan?"

I can feel my eyes growing like cartoon flying saucers. "How'd you know?"

"I know because that prick has hated my ass since we were in Little League, Dr. Z." His words pour out, like he's given this explanation a thousand times. "Soon as I started thinking for myself and wasn't part of his little jock clique, dude started dissing me."

"Well, I hate jocks." Tina hurls a rock. It rattles against the bleachers.

Matthias shoots her a look that reminds me I'm still a stranger here, like in *The Invisible Man*.

"No offense, Zack." Tina's voice gets quiet. "Not all jocks. Just the ones who act like asshats."

"I don't have time to hate anybody," Matthias says. "I just mind my own business, unlike dicks like Declan."

Everything he says makes sense, but I'm still not satisfied. I need details. "What about the lunchroom deal? Is that true?"

"I was out of alignment back then, Dr. Z." He looks down at his board. "Didn't have outlets. No music, no skating. Sometimes, I lost control."

"They said you—"

"What? Banged my head on a wall?"

I shrug. "On the cafeteria table, but yeah, close enough."

"Yeah, I did. Got this scar too." He pulls his bangs back and points to a faint white line between his eyes. "And guess what? I still freak out sometimes. Now, I keep it to myself or let it out in a mosh pit."

I feel about two feet tall in the face of all this honesty. "I dunno. Declan just made a big deal of it."

"That guy is a tool, Dr. Z. It doesn't matter that you don't skate—you're a solid person. Here in our scene, we accept people."

His words make me start to tear up, and I stare at the ground to collect myself. It's true. Despite my lack of skating skills, punk cred, or cool clothes, Matthias welcomed me into his circle. We had an understanding, which I broke by repeating Declan's bullshit.

Tina looks up from a slice of pizza. "There are a couple of polo players in my English class. This morning, one pretended to cough and called me 'skater dyke' under his breath. That's the level of maturity we're dealing with."

"That's messed up, Tina," I say. "If they ever do that again—"

"I told them to put on their Speedos and spank each other's asses like they do after games."

"Touché," says Rob.

"Tons of girls like girls and guys like guys," Matthias says. "This is California, not the fucking backwoods. Being a bigot is like the least punk rock thing ever. Has he heard of Harvey Milk?"

I kick at some rocks, embarrassed to be associated with those polo guys who harassed Tina and tried to make my friend look bad. Suddenly, it's imperative Matty, Tina, and even Rob, know where I stand. Mental note: go read up on Harvey Milk.

"We're not all like that," I say, my voice sounding more imploring than expected. "I'm an athlete, just like you guys. I consider skating a real sport."

"That's because it is," Rob says.

I look over at him. "Exactly, man. I told Declan that skating is insanely technical."

Tina stands, jumps on her skateboard, and makes it spin in a half-circle without the tail touching the ground beneath her feet. "Don't sweat it, new dude," she says, looking pleased with her display. "You think we make a habit of hanging out with people we don't like? Matthias says you're cool. That's good enough for me."

"Thanks," I mumble.

"Nice shuv-it, T," Matthias hollers. "Watch this no comply."

Matthias is coming fast with the skate lingo, almost daring me to decipher his words. Across the lot, he's scooping the tail of his board with his back foot while boosting off the ground with the other foot, and I swear there is a hint of blue flame flying from where his wheels connect with the concrete. I feel like an old sports broadcaster who got dropped off at a skating competition, struggling to comprehend what's on display.

"Can I have your other piece?" Rob shouts while pointing at Tina's Tupperware.

"You need to bring food, dummy."

With a screech, Matthias stops in front of me and crouches. From his patch-covered backpack, he retrieves a Ziplock bag containing a sandwich bursting with sprouts. "You dig that Bad Religion album I got you?"

"It's awesome. I like that 'Infected' song."

Amoeba Records. The CD theft. Our unspoken pact.

Hearing Matty talk about our weekend in front of the gang soothes me, like our friendship extends beyond school boundaries, that we're a pair, separate from everyone.

"Good for you, Dr. Z, listening to non-mainstream music."

Basking in Matty's approval, I'm ashamed I even acknowledged what I heard in the locker room. "Those who mind don't matter, and those who matter don't mind," Dad told me once after I reported some playground gossip.

"Forget what Declan said," I tell Matty. "It doesn't matter."

"We're good, Dr. Z."

A few raindrops hit my arm. He's being chill, but I wonder if Matty's still pissed at me. It's hard to get inside his head. What if he locks me out, cuts off our connection? I'd be irate if someone confronted me about a humiliating middle school experience.

Finally, the passing bell rings, the lunchtime enchantment broken. Our group walks in a single-file line. As we cross the field, the raindrops seem to get bigger, just like the guilt I'm carrying. But I know what I have to do: show my new friend that I'm worthy of his generous heart.

TWELVE
PARENTAL HEADLOCK

We're sitting around our dining room table, the same chunky wooden one we've had since I was little, and Mom has prepared a feast: apricot chicken with Brussels sprouts and mashed potatoes on the side. I kick my shoes off and lean back in my chair, which I know Mom hates. But she doesn't call me on that stuff anymore, not since it's been just the two of us.

"Tell me about your day."

"Well, I looked Harvey Milk up on the internet," I say. "Did you know he was the first gay man elected to office in California? The guy's a legend who got assassinated. I can't believe they didn't teach us about him in Tempe."

"The first *openly* gay man," Mom adds, stabbing a rolling sprout with her fork. "That kind of historical omission drove me and your father batty in Arizona."

"I think I'm starting to get the picture."

"So, how's the water polo going?"

OK, how do mothers have the extraordinary ability to get you to talk about what you don't want to? I let my chair legs touch the floor. "Practice was alright, I guess. Until someone on my team started talking crap."

She leans forward, eyes widening. "About you?"

"No. About my friend. Matthias." I cross my arms.

"Mysterious Matthias who I've yet to meet?"

I can feel my eyes rolling into the back of my head. "Yes, that Matthias. And you'll meet him, Mom. Dang."

She tugs the sleeve of her kaftan to avoid her food. "Care to elaborate on what your teammates said?"

"In the locker room, this guy Declan was spouting off about how Matthias went apeshit in middle school. How he got sent to an asylum."

"Asylum is a very outdated term. More likely he—"

"Whatever, Mom. A place for people with problems." I make a pair of air quotes with my fingers and watch her flinch. "Like Dad could have gone to. Anyway, I asked Matthias about it."

"How was that?"

"Uncomfortable. Shitty."

"Why'd you feel you had to bring it up?"

Good question. "I don't know. It seemed like the type of thing a friend should do."

She scrapes the last of her mashed potatoes onto my plate. "I'm proud of you, Zack. But also sad for your coming years of painful travel on the rocky road to adulthood."

"OK, Mom. No need to get dramatic."

"I was only half-joking."

I pick up our plates and walk over to the sink. "The wildest thing is Matty wasn't even that angry. He's a forgiving dude," I say, as I begin rinsing off the dishes.

"People who've had traumatic experiences usually are."

"So, should I call and apologize?"

She shrugs. "You know best. But it makes me happy to see you've made a real connection in such a short time."

Another thing: moms are insightful even when being hella nosy. They get you in a parental headlock by giving advice without *really* giving advice. I've figured it out. I don't want to blow things with my first real Berkeley friend, even if he does have kleptomaniac tendencies and other assorted problems.

I drag the phone to my bedroom and sit on the floor. Then, with a kaleidoscope of butterflies in my stomach, I dial Matthias's number.

One ring. Two rings.

"Hello, who is it?" a boy's voice answers between gulps of air. My guess is that this is Noel, the kid I saw Matty with at City View.

"Is Matthias there?"

He hollers Matthias's name so loud I have to hold the phone receiver away from my ear. "Hold on a minute," the kid says, returning to normal volume.

Beneath the scratchy sound of a hand on a receiver, I hear the-kid-who-is-probably-Noel say in a muffled voice, "I don't know. Someone from school."

"This is Matthias."

"Hey, Matty. It's Zack."

"Dr. Z." He says my nickname in a way that makes me feel like we're the tightest bros of all time again. "Stoked you called. Sorry, man. I was helping Noel with his homework. He's interviewing me about skating for English."

I remember how patient Matthias acted with the kids at the skatepark, and I feel even worse. I wipe a sweaty palm on the bedspread. "Look, Matty. Forget about that crap Declan said. I wish I'd just blown him off. He's a fool."

"Dude, no worries, I'm not gonna shoot the messenger. Plus, it's true. I go off sometimes."

As his last statement sinks in, I remember Dad in his Dodge, armpit sweat collecting on his blue bathrobe, turning the key in the ignition, and driving into the Arizona summer.

"We all go off sometimes, man," I say. "It's no big thing."

Matthias shouts something away from the receiver, then returns to my ear. "I should get back to Noel, I guess," he says. "Hey, come to my house this weekend. We can hang out and hit Gilman. There's a cool show happening."

"Is that someone's house?"

"It's an all-ages punk club, man. Gilman is legendary."

I'm such an idiot. Gilman is the club's *name*, not just a street. "Sounds awesome. I'll get your address and everything at school."

"You know it."

He's so gracious, which makes me feel even more like a bag of turds. "Matty, sorry again for that bullshit about sixth grade—"

"Dr. Z, you don't have to apologize anymore. I'm always straight with my friends, and I can tell you're the same." He says it softly, but I take it as a warning. Don't push him.

After I hang up, I observe myself in the closet mirror: boring-ass jock in preppy pants, shirt, and imitation skate shoes. I mess up my hair, so I look more like the singer from Sugar Ray. Shitballs, I need better clothes by this weekend for this Gilman place.

"Mom, can you drive me to Goodwill?" I yell.

"You know I don't like talking through the wall," she says from my doorway. "And Goodwill? We're not rich, but we can do better than that. Let me take you to the mall."

I plop down on my bed. "Not the mall, Mom. I need some decent clothes. Matthias asked me to go to a show at Gilman."

She furrows her brow. "What is that? I know the street."

"It's a punk club."

"Aah, I see."

After some more coaxing, I get Mom to take me to Goodwill before they close. The place smells like mothballs and old people, but I score a pair of brown Dickies with glue stains on the back pockets and a faded T-shirt that says "Dave's" in old-school cursive.

Unfortunately, my confidence evaporates when I try the stuff on at home. The pants are stiff as cardboard, and the shirt makes me feel like I'm on *The Brady Bunch*. I take a pained look in the mirror. Is this even punk? I need a second opinion.

I find Mom on the couch in sweatpants, poring over a textbook.

"You think this shirt looks cool?"

She gives me a quick once-over before returning to her work. "I'm no expert on what kids are doing, but that looks like something my students would wear."

I'll take that as a compliment. Gilman, here I come. Whatever it is.

THIRTEEN
MEET THE FAMILY

"This isn't a great part of town, Zack."

Mom's driving through South Berkeley to drop me off at Matthias's house, and I appreciate the ride, if not the commentary. The view through my window consists of piles of bricks in front yards, chain-link fences with Beware of Dog signs, and kids running around without supervision. Still, gritty or not, it's not cool to trash my new friend's neighborhood.

"You're the one being freakin' judgmental now, Mom," I say, as I notice a young Black mother helping two toddlers into the backseat of a rusty Chrysler. "I think this area is cool."

She makes a wide right turn onto his street. "Just keep your wits about you, OK?"

We arrive at the address Matthias gave me. An ancient yellow Volkswagen bus sits parked in the driveway. A wall of bumper stickers nearly covers its back window. One reads, "Be Kind to Animals, Don't Eat Them." The house is the color of red clay, with a long tear in the screen door and chipped paint exposing decaying wood.

Before she can say anything about the state of the place, I jump out and beeline for the front door, not looking back.

"Have fun!" I hear her yell.

Noel answers the door, dressed exactly like one of Matthias's followers in a Santa Cruz sweatshirt, baggie shorts, and Etnies sneakers.

He invites me inside and screams his brother's name. "He'll be up in a sec," Noel informs me.

The house is warm and smells sweet; something sugary is cooking, which I can't quite place. From below comes the blaring sound of punk rock records—that must be Matthias's room.

"Would you like a waffle, Zack?" A woman with light brown hair pulled into a high ponytail wearing a Food Not Bombs shirt holds a plate with a browned Eggo beneath my nose.

"I'd love to, but I just ate." I rub my stomach for good measure.

She looks disappointed for half a second, then smiles as if she's figured out how to solve a problem that's bothered her for days. "How about *half* a waffle, then?"

Matthias appears in time to save me from a carb coma. "Zack's in water polo training, Mom."

"They smell awesome. Next time—when I'm off-season."

"I'll have it." Noel snaps the waffle off the plate.

"C'mon, Dr. Z, let me show you my lair."

His hair looks like he freshly washed it, and he's shirtless, giving me a closer look at that skeletal torso, bruised and scratched from—I assume—skateboarding. Clusters of pink acne dot both his shoulders, scattered among irregular constellations of freckles. I think of my body as a temple; Matthias treats his like an experimental art exhibit.

I crouch and follow Matthias down a carpeted, circular staircase into a windowless basement suite. Two lava lamps sit on the floor and a stick of incense burns in a wooden holder. Every inch is covered with posters and stickers with names like Christian Hosoi, Ron Allen, John Cardiel, Crass, No Use For A Name, and zillions of others. The stereo is blasting a song about refusing to lie down.

Matthias collapses into a ratty brown beanbag. "This is Face to Face. I keep telling you to get into this band."

I can hardly hear him but nod with enthusiasm. The combo of the music and this dim room is making my heart rate increase and my head bob without my consent. "They're rad."

For one song, I remain standing. Then I realize we're listening to the entire album, so I choose the only spot on the bed not covered by *Thrasher* and *Transworld Skateboarding Magazine* issues or DVDs of *Mouse* and *Video Days*. As one speedy punk tune after another clobbers my eardrums, I get accustomed to the attack and feel myself relax. It's comfy down here, and I can't believe no one's asking Matty to turn his music down.

The CD stops, and Matthias springs up. "You get it now, right?"

"Get what?"

"How amazing Face to Face is." Matthias presses play, and the roaring guitars start up again. "You missed the first couple tracks."

We listen to the opening songs at ear-splitting level, and I wear my best "I'm taking this seriously" face until Matthias turns the stereo down a hair.

"It's the shiznit, right?" Matthias picks up the CD and tosses it at me. "This album makes my nipples hard."

I laugh and steal a look at Matty's chest—his nipples look like regular nipples. Matthias is so secure in himself that he'll say whatever comes to mind. "The band sounds killer," I say.

It used to feel like everyone else experienced music on a deeper level than me, that my ears were defective. A few weeks ago, I thought Face to Face was exactly like Rancid or any of the other bands Matthias raves about. Today, their reckless speed and the singer's pleading tone hooked me. Maybe I *am* getting a punk education.

"Your parents seem chill," I tell him.

"They don't care what I do. You'll meet my pop later when he's back from his ride. He's a bike freak."

Motorcycles are omnipresent in Arizona—except if both your parents are professors. "Seems like everyone had a Harley in Arizona."

Matthias laughs. "My dad does trail riding, like mountain bikes," he says. "Be cool to see him on a hog, though."

I deflate like a polo ball on a thumbtack. Why'd I assume he meant motorcycles?

He slides his finger down a CD stack resembling the Leaning Tower of Pisa. "Where's your dad at, Dr. Z?"

"Back in Arizona or New Mexico or somewhere. Divorce shit. We don't talk much. Two years now."

"That's rough, dude."

"It's fine." I make a triangle on the carpet with my shoe. "It's just me and my mom. She's high-strung but cool."

"My parents argue, but that's no big deal. Divorce is some scary shit. I can't picture them not together."

"Neither could I, but it wasn't like *Divorce Court* or anything. More like my dad is out in the desert soul-searching, and it doesn't involve me." I'm tempted, but I can't open up about my father's mental health, not since Declan dropped that warhead about Matthias in sixth grade.

"Let's take a walk," Matthias says. "I need a smoke. That's one thing my parents are not cool with. Weed's OK, but nicotine is the devil."

"In my house, I'd get disowned for either one."

The natural light makes me squint as we emerge from the shadows of Matthias's basement. Noel bounds across the living room as soon as we're upstairs, dropping his Nintendo 64 controller in the process. "Where you guys going?" he asks. The kid's eyes are so bright it's hard not to wish I had a sibling.

Matthias rustles his brother's hair. "Just walking to the yogurt place. You want something?"

Noel squirms away. "I wanna come."

I shove my hands in my pockets as Matty grabs his stickered skateboard, the totem of his individuality.

"Sorry, little man," Matthias says, opening the screen door. "This is a high-schooler-only outing. I'll catch up with you later, OK? We'll play some *Mortal Kombat Trilogy*."

Noel lets out a throaty wail and slams his hands on his thighs. "I'm hella bored," he whines before stomping out of the room.

Outside, the fresh air energizes me. How long were we down in Matty's quarters? It felt like hours.

"C'mon," Matthias says. "I'll show you the hood."

He clutches his board to his chest like a shield as we walk past a row of run-down houses. They resemble his family's, but worse for the wear. I count seven windows with boards across them.

A couple in Raiders jackets strolls toward us, arm in arm. The guy gives us an up nod, and we step out of the way. His girlfriend's hair smells amazing, like apples. As much fun as I'm having with Matty, I can't help but think how chill a relationship would be. There's my romantic side again, yearning to escape.

As we walk, Matthias starts talking nonstop, way more than at school. Some of his thoughts make sense, but mostly, he's in a conversation with himself. It reminds me of the

Jack Kerouac stream-of-consciousness style Dad told me about.

"You have to be ready for whatever happens at Gilman. Shows get hairy there…mosh pits are no joke…used to skate this street all the time…there were potholes everywhere… they've smoothed it way out…*The Anarchist Cookbook* is a must-read, man…this is Berkeley, the center of the world, hippies, gutter punks, squatters, skaters…no one knows what the government does with our food…keep your eyes and ears open…"

While I half-listen, I have a few epiphanies.

Epiphany One: I like this wild part of Berkeley. I feel loose and free, like no one can find me here.

Epiphany Two: This neighborhood isn't scary, just neglected. My mother is a snob or narrow-minded, at the very least. It's not a requirement that we live near university faculty and rent a place next to Geoff or whoever. We could live here and have a house like in Tempe.

Epiphany Three: Wherever we are—Telegraph Avenue, school halls, the skatepark, his living room—Matthias is at ease. Being around him, I feel cooler by association.

"Sweet shirt," Matthias says, yanking my sleeve.

His praise makes the back of my neck go sweaty. "I went to Goodwill like you said to."

Then, without warning, Matty throws his skate down, jumps on, and takes off down the sidewalk. "Watch me grind this red curb."

I swear I see sparks spraying at the point of contact. He makes me miss wrestling, where I had that confidence. Maybe I'll be that smooth at water polo one day, but I doubt it.

"Where's this special yogurt place?"

"There." Matthias points to the mini-mall across a busy intersection. "Don't underestimate it. People trek from all over to come to Yogurt Madness. They have the dopest flavors."

Matthias waits for a hole in traffic and skates across the street, popping up the curb on the other side. I move stiffly in my Dickies; these pants were not designed for running. With Matty, I always feel like I'm a few steps behind, but I try to keep pace, because there's probably something tasty just around the bend.

FOURTEEN

GUILT-FREE FLAVOR

Above the door of Yogurt Madness is a hand-painted sign of a cartoon with a rainbow soft-serve head and John Lennon glasses, another reminder of Berkeley's psychedelic history. "Guilt-free Flavor," the sign proclaims, right below the mascot. I reach my hand beneath my T-shirt and feel my abdominal muscles for reassurance. Hopefully, frozen yogurt won't pack on the poundage.

We step into fluorescent lighting and freezing, sugary air that raises the hair on my forearms. As I acclimate to the subzero temperature, I notice the girl behind the counter.

She has dark brown skin and green eyes and is wearing an apron covered with political pins of all shapes and sizes: Greenpeace, Amnesty International, and a bunch I don't recognize. A half-dozen butterfly clips keep her billowing curls in place.

I'm smitten.

I step to the counter and covertly look at her tag, which says Zaylee with a flower drawn next to the first letter. The exact first letter as my name; this must be a sign.

"A swirl for you, my lady?" she asks the elderly woman

in front of us, which charms the customer to no end. Zaylees's hair bounces as she spins between taking the order and filling the woman's plastic cup in one smooth movement.

Once the customer dawdles off with her yogurt, Matthias leans over the glass. "What's up, Zaylee?"

I look over at him, balancing on his skateboard like it's a cane, muttering under his breath. This morning, I couldn't wait to see Matthias. Now, all of a sudden, with Zaylee around, I wish he'd skate straight out the door. Am I a fickle friend or what?

She wipes down the front of the yogurt machine without even looking at him. "What do you want?"

"The usual."

Zaylee sighs. "So, every flavor, right?"

"Yup, the whole rainbow of taste stimulation," Matthias says in a mellow guy voice about as convincing as an artificial Christmas tree. "Like in the picture." He points to the cartoon hat on the Yogurt Madness mascot.

I cough into my hand. Taste stimulation? Wow, he's being such a cheeseball around this girl. Matty only brought me here to show off how he knows the super cute, unique person. I'm starting to get the picture. On our own, we're equals. When we're out in the world, he gets to be the sophisticated big-city dude, and I'm the hick.

Zaylee takes a cup and pulls the machine lever. A smooth swirl of yogurt flows out. She twists the cup in an elegant dance, moving from vanilla to chocolate to strawberry, then to what looks like cookies and cream. "What does your friend want?" she asks, with her back to us.

"Dr. Z, what flavor?"

"It's Zack," I say, louder than necessary.

Then, it happens: Zaylee looks over her shoulder straight at me, and I melt like a froyo on an August day in Arizona.

"Zack?" She raises an eyebrow.

My ears are ringing. "Basic chocolate would be great."

I watch Zaylee make my yogurt and try to think of something clever.

"$9.57." She places our orders on the counter and looks at each of us. "Want me to split it?"

"I got this." I pass a ten-dollar bill over the counter. My mom gave me thirty bucks, so I'm feeling flush.

Zaylee makes change and drops it into my hand. I shiver involuntarily as her pink fingernails graze my palm—or maybe it's the frosty room.

Matthias pushes the door open with his shoulder. "Bye, Zaylee."

"Uh-huh," she says under her breath.

Then, just as I'm at the door, I hear Zaylee say in a sweet singsong, "Nice to meet you, Zack."

I freeze but somehow thaw myself out in time to reply. "Same here. I mean, nice to meet you too."

"How do you know her?" I ask Matthias a block later, my mouth numb from the yogurt.

"Zaylee?" Matthias asks. "I used to see her at Emeryville youth dances in junior high. She had a crush on me."

So, that one-of-a-kind being who elevated serving frozen yogurt into an art form had a crush on ratty little Matthias? No chance. Zaylee doesn't look like skating skills would dazzle her. "Does she go to our school?"

"Nah, Bishop O'Dowd," Matthias says with a haughty wiggle. "It's a private school for stuck-up kids. That's why Zaylee acts like she's all that and a bag of chips."

Or maybe you're not her type. Time to drop the subject before I come off as too interested. Even through his aloof act, it's easy to see Matthias was the one infatuated with Zaylee, not the other way around.

And now there are two of us in her fan club.

A beat-up El Camino crawls around the corner, blasting "I Got 5 On It." The bass is cranked so high all the house windows are pulsing in time.

"Luniz," Matty says and waves his arms to the beat. "Hell yeah. They're from Oakland."

I suddenly feel super lame about the yogurt in my hand, so I tilt the cup back and finish the remaining liquid before crumpling it into a strange, contorted shape. It looks sort of like a heart.

We ascend the cracked, plum-colored steps to Matthias's house, and he lets himself in.

Here's the deal: I may lack experience with girls, but I pay attention when my intuition barks marching orders. As of today, my prime directive is to return to Yogurt Madness and get Zaylee's phone number—*without* coming off like a creepazoid in the process. To do that, I can't have Matthias around.

But I can deal with that later. We're back in his domain now, and I need Matty's expertise. After all, I'm going on my first punk rock adventure tonight, and he's my tour guide.

FIFTEEN
GILMAN

Back in his downstairs hideaway, Matthias is in a frenzy, tossing CDs from hand to hand, playing me song after song by bands with names like NOFX, Screeching Weasel, and Sick Of It All, even a few Green Day numbers for good measure. ("Just their first few releases," he says, "before they sold out.")

Time is elastic down here, but after what seems like hours, I hear his mom's voice shout about dinner. Before we return to the upstairs world to grub down, Matthias explains that his family doesn't eat meat.

"But didn't I see you scarf down a burger last week during lunch?"

"That was a veggie burger, Dr. Z. Meat is murder." He points to a torn poster with four black and white repeating images of a soldier with the same phrase scrawled on his helmet.

Apparently, the whole Alexander clan gathers for an old-school family dinner every night. Matty's mother serves us spaghetti with red sauce and garlic bread sticks, everything vegetarian, as warned. The pasta has a yellowish tint, which is a tad hippieish, but at least there's plenty to go around.

Matthias's father is a broad-shouldered man's man sporting a beard with plenty of gray. He's wearing red Converse All Stars and has his jean cuffs rolled up. "You guys ready to head out soon?" He bangs his head and mimes strumming a guitar. It's nerdy but sweet.

I look to Matthias for a cue but can't catch his eye. He's got both elbows on the table and is shoveling a breadstick into his mouth. "Dang, Pop," he says, crumbs flying everywhere, "you're more pumped to drive us than we are to go."

"Punk rock is good for the soul," Matthias's father says. "Get some energy out." He burps loudly, inching his seat back from the table.

"Oscar," says Matthias's mother.

"Everyone belches, Cynthia."

In response, Noel emits a perfect burp of his own. Matthias gives him a high five.

"Zack, did Matthias tell you I was into punk rock?" Oscar asks.

I want to leap out of my plastic-cushioned seat and hug Oscar and Cynthia for being so carefree and accepting. Wonder how I could get the Alexanders to adopt me. "Truthfully, I'm still new to punk—"

"Loved the Clash," Oscar interrupts. "I even saw the Sex Pistols last show." He points his index finger at Matthias, then at me. "Did you know it was in San Francisco?"

Noel laughs into his napkin. "Ooh, you said Sex Pistols, Dad."

Matthias looks to the ceiling. "You've also told us that story a billion times."

"Punk and politics are deeply intertwined," Oscar says. "What do I always say?"

"Angela Davis is punk rock," Matthias answers.

"Damn right she is." He points at a vintage framed poster that reads, "Free Angela Davis Now!"

Angela Davis—another person I need to learn about. "I'm embarrassed, but I don't know the Clash or the Sex Pistols," I say. "Mostly, I've learned about punk from Matthias."

"I'm weaning him off that radio dreck." Matthias reaches for another breadstick. My friend's metabolism is a marvel. I could never eat that many carbs without keeling over and falling asleep.

Oscar tousles Matthias's hair. "Keep hanging around this guy, and you'll get your full dose of originality, that's for sure. Right, Cynthia?"

"Well, he didn't get his fashion sense from me," Cynthia replies. "I did my part with politics, though. It's a Berkeley mandate."

"In sixth grade, Matthias came home from the barbershop with a pink mohawk," Oscar says. "We knew we had a free thinker that minute."

An image of Declan shit-talking Matthias in the locker room passes through my mind. Sixth grade must have been quite a year: a mohawk and a breakdown.

Cynthia picks up Noel's plate, then Oscar's. "And he still makes time to teach his brother to skateboard."

"Zack moved here from Arizona," Matthias interjects. "Dr. Z was a star wrestler, and he's on the water polo team now. My man can play any sport."

He's praising me now, but he was a complete shithead about Zaylee. Man, friendship is complex.

"Polo, huh?" Oscar reaches across the table and squeezes my bicep. "No surprise you've got some guns on you. Bet the girls notice those."

I blush and maneuver my last bit of spaghetti onto my fork. My muscle aches a bit where Mr. Alexander grabbed it;

he's got a Kung Fu Grip.

"You two get ready," Cynthia says. "We'll clean up."

Matthias pushes his chair back and darts from the table, leaving me with his family. With an apologetic shrug, I exit and descend into the underworld.

I find him pacing the floor with a Subhumans CD case in his hand. A singer with a thick British accent is howling the word "no" at me like I'm the source of every bit of disappointment he's faced in his entire life.

"So, there are things you need to know about Gilman," Matthias says.

Time for another lesson. "OK, what's the 411?"

He pulls a crumpled card from his wallet. "They'll ask you for a membership card at the door. They do the same thing with everyone. You only have to buy it once, but no one remembers to bring it."

"I've got money for one."

"And don't be surprised that it's hella trashed. That's what Gilman looks like."

"Trashed?"

Matthias scoops a chewed-up Nerf football from the floor. "It's punk rock," he says. "You'll get it when you see it."

Meep mee mee meep, meep meep meep.

The sound of a car horn cuts through the chaotic music. Matthias tosses me the Nerf and claps both hands. "Show time, go time."

We race upstairs and pile into the backseat of the family's VW Bus. I remember Matthias telling me his dad was a school bus driver. Guess it makes sense they have one of their own.

The VW is the final piece of their punk hippie family puzzle—old leather seats and an interior that smells like graham crackers. Feels like going back in time to the 1970s. I wonder how long the family has owned this artifact.

Once we're buckled in, Oscar cranks the stereo. The sound is tinny and piercing. "You know this one?" he hollers at me.

Matthias leans in between his dad and the empty passenger seat. "Duh, Pop. It's 'I Fought the Law.'"

Oscar smiles, pounding the steering wheel to the beat. "The Clash, Zack. The only band that matters."

"Sounds like a Western movie," I reply, and Oscar laughs.

We zoom down the freeway with this angry, hellacious music shooting at us like audio gunfire, and I gaze out at the city at dusk. The clear blue sky is fading into black as we pass rolling hills and endless apartments. All around us, the East Bay is changing into its evening wear.

I look at my friend beside me and decide to let him off the hook for being a dickhead in front of Zaylee. Instead, I close my eyes and appreciate this closeness, the family vibes.

Our surroundings get increasingly industrial until we eventually come upon a few dozen punk rockers with dyed hair, chains, and ripped clothing standing in a long line. The VW stops sharply. We've arrived at 924 Gilman Street.

"Have fun," Oscar yells from the window like he's dropping us off at summer camp. As he drives off, I still hear the Clash playing in the distance, the singer yelling something about a rock and roll world.

Matthias flashes a salute at his dad and hustles across the street. I follow. It's weird seeing him out without his skateboard.

Once we're in line, Matthias leans in so close to my ear that I smell the garlic on his breath from dinner. "The shows start early because it's all ages."

"Got it."

Unlike Telegraph, the skatepark, or anywhere else we've gone together, Matthias doesn't know anyone here. All ages or not, this is an older, tougher crowd. My Goodwill outfit might be a slight upgrade, but I'm a straight-up preppy here. Matthias blends in better, but not by much. We look like pathetic high schoolers.

Who knew there were so many kinds of punk rockers? It's super diverse, just like the East Bay. One Filipino girl in front of us in line has two thin green Mohawks and a ring between her eyes. A tall African American guy is working the door. He's wearing a shirt with the words "The Selecter" on it. A fitting name for someone letting people into a club, I guess.

"Is The Selecter a band I should know?" I ask Matthias.

"They're two-tone ska from England, and they're outstanding."

Mental note: punk and hip-hop aren't the only styles I need to check out. There is also ska. There are so many details about underground music. It's like learning wrestling stats.

Soon, we reach the front of the line. I look to my left and see a stenciled, spray-painted sign on the wall that reads: NO ALCOHOL, NO DRUGS, NO VIOLENCE, NO STAGE-DIVING, NO DOGS, NO FUCKED-UP BEHAVIOR, NO RACISM. NO MISOGYNY/SEXISM, NO HOMOPHOBIA, $2 MEMBERSHIP

Five bucks with a membership card. Seven bucks without," the door guy says. "Your membership card's valid for a year."

I hand over my money.

"Have a good time," he says, giving me my change.

Matthias flashes his card and pays.

And then we're inside. I've never seen anything like this

immense, grimy warehouse filled with punk kids. Ceiling fans are spinning, blowing cold air on the crowd, loud music blares from speakers, and stickers and graffiti cover every surface. It's perfect chaos.

"Cool, we didn't miss anything," Matthias says. "First band is still setting up." He points at a pack of kids in ripped jeans lugging amps onto the stage. They don't seem much older than us.

Onstage, a tall, slender girl with her back to the crowd assembles a blue drum set. She has fuchsia-colored hair in two small ponytails, one on either side of her head. She turns to look at the gathering audience, and I catch a terrified expression crossing her face.

"You know this band?" I ask Matthias. "They look young."

He walks over to a flyer hanging from a single staple on the wall. "They're first." His finger follows a trail of band logos until it reaches the bottom. "They're called Kitten Cavalry."

"Funny name."

"They'll be good. It's almost impossible to get a gig at Gilman. Even as an opener."

The guitarist plugs in and hits a clanging, distorted chord. The sound is so abrasive I can't imagine listening to it for any longer than necessary, but I steel myself for the imminent onslaught.

"They're starting." Matthias runs toward the stage where bodies are emerging from the shadows, from every corner of the club, to create a human wall in front of the band.

The drummer smacks her snare drum a few times and hits a shrill cymbal crash. It isn't as painful on my ears as the guitar, so maybe there's a chance I'll survive the set.

There are only three members. The guitar player wears a backward baseball cap, and his shirt says Pansy Division, another unfamiliar band name. The bassist is a chubby girl in cutoff jeans with a tiny, red sparkle guitar. After huddling with her bandmates, she counts the band in with a squeaky voice, and they're off.

Kitten Cavalry is fucking loud but better when all the instruments are playing together. The sound waves emitting from the amps feel like they're heating up the room. Kids are spazzing out, arms and legs flailing like they're possessed by malevolent spirits. Come to think of it, they're thrashing around like Matthias does. So this is where he gets his moves.

"This is queercore," Matthias shouts into my ear. "They're a gay and lesbian band. Very cool."

Queercore—you learn a new word every day. All three members of Kitten Cavalry sing, or more accurately, holler with gusto. The guitarist keeps running back to the drummer and returning to the microphone in perfect time to sing the following line. Punk has more in common with sports than you'd think.

They stop for a second, and the squeaky-voiced bass player walks up to her microphone; she handles most of the between-song talking. "This is called 'Mommy Dearest.' One, two, three, four." And they're off again, blasting out their loudest, fastest song yet. The drummer plays at incredible speed without breaking a sweat. She also chews gum, even while singing backups.

People start shoving, and a hole emerges in the crowd. Kids run across the circle, bisecting it at every angle, throwing free-form hand gestures, and performing improvised dance routines.

"Looks like we've got ourselves a pit." Matthias's eyes are dancing with the same fire as earlier today when he was playing me songs. He lives for this insanity. As the pit gets wilder, my method of defense is to cross my arms and tense my whole body.

Soon, it's a game of pushing sweaty punks off when they slam against me. The lifting and polo pay off; I barely budge. The controlled chaos of moshing reminds me of a wild game. Only there are no teams; it's everyone for themselves.

After less than twenty minutes, Kitten Cavalry finishes. The bassist says, "Thanks," and that's it—no big bows or throwing drumsticks into the crowd like in an MTV video.

Seconds later, the next band is dragging its gear onstage. There are more members and not a girl in sight. Black baseball hats with embroidered skate company patches, black Ben Davis pants, tattoos on their arms, even on their necks.

"I've heard of these guys," Matthias says, hopping from foot to foot like a kid waiting in line at the amusement park. "They're called Rivet. I saw their album at Amoeba. Someone said they sound like Good Riddance."

Rivet is louder and angrier than Kitten Cavalry. The number of people in the club multiplies in minutes, and the crowd gets rowdier. There's now a designated circle with people on the outside, their arms ready to reach out and keep people in the pit from spilling out into the regular crowd. Mom would not like seeing me in this environment. Guaranteed.

As I witness the anarchy, my thoughts drift to something we discussed in world history last year: self-determination. It's impressive how self-governing this place is. Beneath all the grit, everything feels under control.

Matthias is hyped up to ten, as usual. While Rivet plays, he runs into the middle of the fray and stumbles around. Watching the bodies flinging each other around, the "No Violence" sign on the door starts to seem hypocritical.

The room is hotter now and reeks like a combination of

body odor and hairspray. After a half-hour, Rivet ends with a long buildup. The red-faced singer yells, "See you next time, Gilman," and the pit clears.

"C'mon," Matthias says. "Everyone goes outside between bands."

I follow his lead, unsure about what happens next, except it will probably be outside my comfort zone.

SIXTEEN
THE ALLEY

A group of punks assembles in front of Gilman, smoking cigarettes and acting tough. It's a wild scene, and I'm a polo player out of water, so it's safest to stick by Matthias's side, even though he's still acting like he's in the middle of the pit, pushing at invisible people.

Matty bums a cigarette from a guy with green spikes pointing out of his head.

"You want a light?" the guy asks. He's got a baby face and can't be much older than me. Wonder what his parents think of his hair.

Matthias inhales, blows the smoke out, then passes the cigarette to me. All my life, I've seen cancer commercials and listened to lectures from teachers. Still, suddenly, I'm sucking on the end of the cigarette like a shitty actor. It feels like a tiny red line starting in my throat and traveling to the center of my chest, where the smoke sits and irritates the tissue. Every fiber of my being wants to cough, but I hold it in until the impulse subsides.

You've done it now, Coleman. You're a bad kid. There's no turning back.

While I stare at my shoes and pretend to take another drag, Matthias moves over to a pair of punk girls. This feels like a party I didn't plan on attending. Miguel passes through my mind. How wild and unpredictable my life would seem to him, how far removed from our sheltered Tempe world.

"Meet my friend," Matthias says. One of the girls has bright red hair, shaved everywhere except for the bangs and little pieces on the sides. The other looks like a heavy-set vampire in all black with long eggplant-colored locks and tons of eye makeup. She's holding a flask in her hands. Wait, didn't the sign say no drinking?

Matthias ushers me over. "This is Dr. Z."

"Zack, actually."

Matthias puts his hand on the shoulder of the girl with the wild hair. "This is Mary and..." He snaps his fingers.

"Dana," she says in a Valley Girl voice, which clashes with her clothing.

"Dana has some Jack Daniels." Matthias raises his fingers to his mouth. "Don't tell Gilman security. They'll throw us out of here."

She passes a flask to Matthias, who takes a deep swig. "Damn, that's good."

"Give it here," Mary says in an irritated voice.

I'm also annoyed but for a different reason. I have a terrible feeling about seeing Matthias drunk.

"Hey," a big dude with glasses shouts. "You can't drink in front of Gilman. Go somewhere else."

"Piss off, narc," Mary spits.

This is getting rowdier than I thought it would.

"Mary," Dana half-whispers. "Let's just go to the alley."

The girls shuffle off, and Matthias follows them like a puppy.

"How do you know these two?" I ask.

"I don't," he replies. His breath smells like liquor.

"Matty, let's head back inside."

"In a minute, Desert Rat." He tries to catch up with the girls. "Wait up, Dana."

Now, we're all standing in an alley that's dark, cold, and smells of urine and damp cardboard.

"You want a drink, buffed guy?" Mary asks, pointing the flask in my direction.

"I'm fine."

"You are pretty fine—for a preppy." Dana slinks over and rubs my arm. Matthias and Mary are making out against the alley wall. She has one leg up, and her fishnet stockings are showing. Mary is sighing, and Matthias is breathing heavily like he's in a teen sex movie, which is both exciting and revolting. From the club, you can hear the loud thump of the bass guitar.

"Ignore them." Dana scratches the back of my neck. "Pay attention to me." Then, she's kissing me, her mouth opening wide and tongue going everywhere. She tastes of booze and mints. Wait, is that a wadded-up piece of gum? Yes, it sure is.

Dana moans softly, rubbing the inside of my thigh. "You're a cutie, aren't you," she whispers.

In my peripheral vision, our respective friends are going at it hotter and heavier by the moment. There's a lot of grunting going on. I guess they're inspiring Dana because she starts grinding against me and kissing harder.

"Dana, let's go." Mary's voice sounds even more annoyed than when she wanted the booze. "The next band is starting. Also, I'm kinda wasted."

"Fine," Dana says, pulling away and fixing her hair. "Later, Muscles."

As the girls walk toward the light at the end of the alley, Matthias smiles at me. "Isn't Gilman amazing?"

"Yes, it is." Even though Dana is kind of cheesy, I'm sorry to see her go, especially after the most serious makeout session of my life.

Matthias starts in a wobbly line in the direction of the club entrance.

I grab him by his shoulder. "Are you drunk?"

He turns to look at me, only half his face showing in the moonlight. "Do I seem drunk? Punk rock, bro."

We slip back inside, where four guys in sweatpants and baggy black shirts are playing. They sound crunchier and less catchy than the earlier bands. The mosh pit is bigger and rowdier than before. Matthias doesn't hop in this time; he just watches in a daze.

"These guys are totally metal," he tells me. "Not my deal, but they're OK."

Dana is standing on the far right of the stage, fixated on the band. Our eyes meet briefly, but she ignores me. Cigarettes, making out with drunk girls in alleys? This is not the old Zack.

Matthias punches me in the shoulder. "My pop will be down the street soon, and he's never late."

We leave Gilman and walk to our meeting place. For all his bravado, fast talking, drinking, and skating, Matthias is just like me. He doesn't want anyone to see his parents drop him off or pick him up.

"You two have fun?" Oscar asks as we get in the backseat.

"Most definitely." Matthias curls himself into a ball beside me like a small child.

"Totally," I say, closing my eyes as Oscar pulls the VW onto the freeway. Sometimes, it's easier to pretend you're asleep—fewer questions from adults. In my mind's eye, the evening replays like a movie—from Kitten Cavalry to

Matthias's spastic slam dancing to Dana's boozy kisses. What a night.

Oscar drops me off at home, where I open the door as quietly as possible.

"Did you have a nice time?"

"Yeah, Mom. I'll tell you about it tomorrow."

My head hits the soft, fresh pillow, and the loud ringing in my ears creates a backdrop for images of me and Dana fooling around in the alley. Then, feeling weirdly guilty, I swap out drunk Dana with Zaylee serving frozen yogurt—cool, independent, and funny. I fall asleep smiling.

SEVENTEEN
ROLE REVERSAL

I give Mom my censored Gilman show report on Sunday morning—no slamming, alcohol, or back alley make-out session. Luckily, she seems distracted, so I don't have to go into great detail. Later, when I find her thumbing through an issue of *Scientific American*, I decide it's time to put my secret plan to see Zaylee into action.

"What are you reading?"

"It's an article about gene therapy for cancer," she says, "and how genes can theoretically arrest tumor growth."

"Sounds intriguing."

"Oh, it is. This could be a crucial turning point in treating AIDS."

After that intense response, I feel highly inappropriate changing the subject, but you gotta do what you gotta do.

"Think I can get a ride to the yogurt place near Matthias's house Saturday afternoon?"

OK, it's a white lie, but I don't feel like revealing my romantic intentions to my mother. Hopefully, Saturdays are Zaylee's regular shift, and I won't be wasting the favor.

She looks up from her reading. "Sure, kiddo. I love that

you're making friends. You should invite this Matthias over soon."

"Yeah, I'll do that." My heart is pounding; it worked.

She rearranges her legs, so both are beneath her. "Zack, there's something I've been meaning to tell you, and it hasn't been the exact right moment."

Fear washes over me. Have I been discovered? Maybe my clothes reeked of smoke after Saturday night. "What's up?" I try to sound casual.

"You know Geoff from next door?" She removes her glasses, which only happens before addressing an uncomfortable topic.

"I met him when we moved in."

"Well, we began talking while I was picking up our mail the other day. Turns out he's a very nice, intelligent man."

No wonder Mom was barely paying attention when I told her about the punk club; she had this conversation on her mind. I let her ramble while wearing my best "interested son" look.

"Since then, Geoff and I have been eating lunch together on campus." She pauses and takes a deep breath. "I wanted to let you know we might do something in the evening one of these days."

Mom returns her glasses to her face and straightens them on the bridge of her nose, clearly happy to have made this revelation. The silence is a signal that it's my turn to talk.

"I've only spoken with Geoff for a second here and there, but he seems cool." Thank God, this isn't a conversation about punk rock, booze, or smoking.

Her forehead is scrunched up, but she's smiling. "I want you to know I'm not rushing into anything. Your Dad is still—"

"Mom, I get it. You're going on a date with Geoff." I stand up. "I'm happy for you."

She looks like she's going to cry. "How'd you get so grown-up? Don't answer that. I'm so proud of you for dealing with all these changes."

I squeeze her shoulder. "I'm proud of you too, Mom."

Since Dad's been out of the picture, sometimes I feel like we've reversed roles, and I'm the one offering the approval. It can be embarrassing, but I'm not complaining. After all, you only get one Mom, and she just agreed to take me to meet my dream girl—even if neither one of them knows it.

———

I'm still secreting punk rock from my pores when homeroom comes around on Monday.

"Looks like you got up to something this weekend."

I lift my head from where it's been resting on my forearms to see Danny Chang directly in front of me. "What makes you say that?"

He balances on the corner of my desk and twirls a pencil haphazardly. "Dude, your eyes are as red as mine."

Uh-oh. You know you're in trouble when Danny notices your sorry state. A single cigarette two days earlier wouldn't make me need Visine—would it?

"Nah, I'm just tired," I say. "I went to Gilman to see some bands on Saturday."

Danny looks like he's stitching his thoughts together behind the veil of his marijuana haze. "Must have been out with your new buddy, Matthias," he says finally, with an unexpected edge.

"Yeah, Matthias took me. You been to Gilman?"

He slides off my desk and runs both hands through his shaggy hair. "You know what, man? I never have. Weird, right?"

Images flicker across my mind like an old filmstrip: my

first glimpse of the graffiti-covered interior, the crowd raging to Rivet, the green spike guy. "Gilman was amazing." It does feel satisfying to have done something in the East Bay that Danny hasn't.

"That's cool," Danny says without meeting my eyes. The bell rings, and we drift apart into the hallway, absorbed by the horde.

At lunch, behind the bleachers, Matthias and I observe an unspoken code of silence about the weekend until Tina starts asking questions. I remember how she said her parents are majorly religious and won't let her go to shows or engage in anything remotely fun outside school.

"What bands played?" Tina asks.

Matthias closes his eyes like he's trying to remember the millions of concerts he's been to since Saturday night. "Rivet played. They were pretty sick."

Tina bites her bottom lip and pulls her beanie down. "I read about them in *Maximum Rocknroll*. They're supposed to be killer live."

"Kitten Cavalry, too," I add. "They were mostly girls."

Tina glares at me. "Never heard of them." Her look seems to say, "Why did this newbie jock get to go to Gilman while I was stuck at home?"

Rob puts his arm around Tina's shoulder; she brushes him away. "There'll be other shows," he says.

"Yeah, your parents will loosen up eventually, Tina," Matthias says in the same sweet voice he uses with Noel.

Tina looks off at the football field. "Yeah, maybe."

"Could be worse," Rob says, kicking at gravel and bottle caps in front of him. "At least your parents don't get shit-faced and say you're a waste of space."

No one utters a word. We just watch Matthias do tricks and eat our lunches in silence.

Tina and Rob's crappy home situations make me feel

incredibly lucky. Mom trusts me and gives me freedom. As for my dad, his abuse was strictly self-directed. He never told me I was worthless, that's for sure.

I look from Tina to Rob to Matty and think of my dad. We've all got our demons, don't we?

EIGHTEEN
HOW BIZARRE

Saturday afternoon eventually arrives, and I remind Mom she agreed to drop me off at Yogurt Madness to meet Matthias. Thankfully, she talks nonstop during the drive, so I don't have to compound my lie with even more bullshit.

"You know, the sooner you get a license, the sooner you can take control of your social life," she tells me as we pull into the lot.

"Point taken. You're not my chauffeur." I scramble out the side door to avoid any more unsolicited advice. "I'll call if I need a ride home."

Dad used to drive me to matches and on his errands while giving me dumbed-down lectures. His sturdy presence behind the wheel made driving seem fun, like a badge of honor. Currently, it's another responsibility that freaks me the hell out.

Mom drives off, and I'm left standing at the mini-mall; my palms are sweaty, and my stomach is spinning like a blender on ten. I walk over to the window of Yogurt Madness, where I see Zaylee counting change at the cash register. A minor miracle—she's here. Now to make a smooth entrance.

A lady in a GUESS sweatshirt brushes by me, ushering in her two kids, which should give me some cover. No luck. The door dings loudly as she pushes it open. Zaylee catches my eye and smiles.

"Welcome to Yogurt Madness."

So much for the stealth approach.

My mind spits questions like a slot machine dumping quarters: Will she remember me? Does this shirt look too preppy? Is there a chance to make this drop-by look unplanned? *Quit tripping.* Just walk in, buy a frozen yogurt, and see what transpires.

While the brats ask to try every flavor in the store, I try to concoct an opening line. Luckily, Zaylee swoops in before anything stupid comes out of my mouth.

"You're that skater dude's friend, right? Matthew or whatever. He comes in here every Saturday."

What if Matthias waltzes through the door right now, wild-eyed and flipping his hair around? "Matthias. We're friends—but I'm not a skater or anything."

Didn't Matthias tell me Zaylee goes to a fancy Catholic school? Athletics hold some extra weight at those bourgeois places. "I play water polo for the Berkeley High Yellowjackets. I'm Zack."

"I remember you, Zack. We both have 'z' names. That doesn't happen every day." She rests both arms on the yogurt case and leans in to place her chin directly across from me. "Water polo—cool. So, what brings you around today? Meeting up with your skater pal?"

The way Zaylee is looking at me is giving me severe chest palpitations—more than the most intense session of lap swimming this year. "No, I'm hanging by myself. Just wanted to get a chocolate-peanut-butter-coconut swirl." My voice sounds as horrible as my made-up excuse.

"A triple swirl it is, then." Zaylee pushes off the glass and turns around. "So, you're a polo player," she says, maneuvering the cup as the humming machine dispenses the three yogurt flavors.

I search my barren brain for something interesting to advance the conversation. "I'll be starting at our first game."

She hands me my yogurt. "OK, now you're just showing off."

I pay and spoon some yogurt from the side of the cup, attempting to avoid damaging the immaculate twist Zaylee created. What does that Nike ad say? Just do it? "I was wondering if you might want to hang out sometime. Maybe today, after you close?"

Zaylee hands me my change and reaches over to wipe down the glass with a rag. "Sure, meet me here at 5:15." She points her thumb toward the broom closet. "I have to clean up at the end of the day."

A song called "How Bizarre" is playing through the shop's tinny speakers. What's bizarre is how amazing this moment feels, way more satisfying than scoring during a scrimmage or beating my personal lifting best.

"Awesome, I'll see you later."

There's a single tiny table in the shop by the door, but there's no way I'll sit in Zaylee's presence and eat yogurt like a nerd.

"Sounds good, Zack."

Double whammy: hearing Zaylee use my name and seeing her smile at me. That grin is beyond captivating—like she knows a secret and is daring me to figure it out. I leave Yogurt Madness in a hurry while attempting to play it cool.

Hopefully, Matthias doesn't skate by; that would be a disaster of epic proportions. He was so harsh about Zaylee, but I know better—she can't stand him. Last week, impressing Matty was my primary focus in life. How quickly things change.

Once I'm securely out of Zaylee's line of vision, I throw the froyo straight into a trash can and break into a run while "How Bizarre" loops in my head.

NINETEEN
A SENSITIVE JOCK

With some time until Zaylee closes Yogurt Madness, I hit Bob's Sports Card Emporium at the mini-mall and wander the musty racks. Since I was a kid, I've loved getting lost in the rows of sports history, all those legacies and dreams filling every square inch. These kinds of places make me wonder what the future holds for me. Will I be commemorated on a card or a poster? That would be sick.

Then, right on the dot, I return to find Zaylee locking the front door like an actual adult employee. It's an impressive and intimidating sight to someone like me who's never even held a part-time job.

"What'd you get up to?" she asks

"Nothing much. Just hung around Bob's and checked out cards."

"Wow, you're brave. That place reeks of mildew and Pine-Sol. I don't think I've ever seen anyone under sixty go in there."

Damn it. Zaylee thinks that place is for losers. "I was looking for this one rare—"

"Relax, I was joking. You want to drive somewhere?"

"That'd be cool. But I don't drive yet."

"Good thing one of us does." Zaylee beeps her car key toward a tan Kia parked in front of Yogurt Madness. "I'll take you to see my school if you want."

Minutes later, I'm on the freeway with a girl whose car smells like strawberry air freshener. Zaylee has a multi-disc CD changer on shuffle, so it's Fugees, Gin Blossoms, and Toni Braxton. Honestly, it's refreshing to hear something other than punk rock, to listen for pure enjoyment, not flip off society.

Zaylee rolls down our windows, and soon my hand is dangling in the evening breeze. This feels like ultimate freedom, far beyond pinning an opponent or making a goal. Just mellow sounds, a beautiful night, and the most incredible girl I've ever met.

She's tapping her fingers on the wheel to Hootie and the Blowfish; I recognize the singer's deep voice. Matthias would mock the shit out of this song, call it "commercial crapola." Well, I'm here, and he's not.

"What year are you, Zack?"

Uh-oh. I hold my breath before replying. "Sophomore."

"Wow."

I draw back my hand from outside. "I mean—"

"It's fine. You seem mature, that's all." Zaylee says. "I'm a senior."

Of course, Zaylee's a senior; she's got a car, a job, her own style, tons of confidence. Somehow, in all my detailed daydreams, our ages never came up. Hope this won't be a deal-breaker.

Seems like an opportune time to shift the conversation away from me. "What made you get a job at Yogurt Madness?"

"It has that cute old-school vibe," she replies.

I think of Matthias and how he hyped the place up to me. "Yeah, the yogurt is amazing."

"Plus, South Berkeley is an important historically Black neighborhood," she says. "I mean, the Black Panthers were active there in the '60s and '70s."

"Wow. I didn't know that." There's so much I need to learn about my new city.

"Here we are." Zaylee pulls her car into a spot in front of Bishop O'Dowd High School. The place is enormous, with manicured lawns and imposing buildings.

I close the passenger door behind me and take in the campus. "Your school is deluxe."

Zaylee stares straight ahead. "It's big, that's for sure. Twenty acres or something. It's been here since the '50s."

"You like going here?"

"It's pretty white and sheltered by Oakland standards."

"Like, most of the student body is white? Berkeley High isn't like that at all."

"You go to school in the real world. Let's just say I'm used to being one of the few Black students in my year," she says and starts walking. "My parents forced me onto the private school path, but I've never belonged here."

I don't know how to respond. "It must be weird."

"It gets embarrassing when kids tokenize me." Zaylee makes a motion like her head is exploding. "Do you know how often I've had to say I prefer Matchbox Twenty to Tupac?"

"My guess would be a lot?"

"You'd be right." She laughs. "But it's more than the lack of diversity. Let's just say, the opportunities for activism are *sorely* limited."

"Like volunteering and stuff?" I point at the colorful assortment of buttons on her worn-in denim jacket. Before tonight, I'd only seen her in her Yogurt Madness apron.

"There are thousands of important causes. Berkeley's been the center of so much radical change," Zaylee says, waving her arms around her. "This place, on the other hand, is stuck in the past. And not in a good way."

As she leads me through the deserted campus, I feel like I'm in a romantic movie sequence. This stuff doesn't happen to me. Hooking up at Gilman was a wild exception. In real life, the extent of my dating experience consists of a few crushes and clumsy kisses.

I try to get a look at Zaylee without her noticing. Now that I know her age, everything about her screams senior—the confident way she communicates, her causes, the way her body fills out her clothes. It's like she's halfway out the door to college already, and I'm falling hopelessly behind by the nanosecond.

"It sucks that it's so apolitical here," I say, hoping she'll notice the flashy vocab. "But you probably have tons of friends."

"Not really." Zaylee kicks at a dirt clump. "The kids are OK, I guess. I've known most since grade school, so there isn't a lot of mystery."

"Mystery?"

"As far as dating or whatever. Everyone's like a sibling." She looks into my eyes to make sure I'm paying attention. "Berkeley High must be different."

"Don't know. I moved here from Arizona at the end of the summer."

"Where in Arizona?"

"Tempe, but I've stopped saying that. No one in California even knows where that is."

Zaylee breaks away and takes a set of steep cement steps two at a time. "Tempe is near Phoenix, right?" she shouts over her shoulder. "My family drove through there one summer. It felt like walking across the surface of the sun."

She looks down at me from the top of the stairs. "But that's all I remember."

I race up the stairs to catch up. "The hellish heat is all anyone remembers, but you get used to it."

Zaylee pushes open the school's colossal front door, which, for some reason, is unlocked.

"They must have student groups or something," she explains, reading my mind. "A lot of stuff goes on here during the weekend."

Once we're inside, she rests her shoulder against a glass door. Through it, I see an auditorium.

"So, Arizona to California," Zaylee begins, "that must have taken some acclimation."

"My mom teaches science at Cal. Both my parents are professors." I toss off the last detail. "People say I'm brainy for a jock, whatever that means."

"Your mom teaches at UC Berkeley?" She runs her arm along the wall while she continues walking. "Ask her if she knows June Jordan, who founded Poetry for the People. That program is the bomb."

"Actually, my father is a poet."

"A scientist mother and a poet dad." She pushes herself off the glass and walks away, leaving me looking at my reflection. "You're full of surprises, Zack. For a sophomore."

This place is very dreamlike, like a TV version of a school. We stumble through halls plastered with colorful posters for dances and football games. Bishop O'Dowd seems, for lack of a better word, wholesome. Or else I've been spending so much time with Matthias at spots like Gilman that I'm getting accustomed to grime.

We pass through another door, and we're outside again. The sun's nearly down now, and it's chillier. Zaylee leads me across the football field until we reach a fence at what looks like the edge of the school.

"Where are you taking me?"

"Hop the fence, and I'll show you someplace special."

It's a decent size fence, but Zaylee scales it with little effort.

"Nice form." I find my footing and hoist myself over. The fence rattles as I hit the soft earth on the other side.

We push through crowded bushes and emerge in a cleared-out area with neatly arranged wooden planters. It's like a tiny farm, complete with half-open bags of manure, a few shovels, and an ancient wheelbarrow propped against a rickety red shed.

"Welcome to my secret garden," Zaylee says like she's proclaiming ownership of a country she discovered.

"This is straight out of *The Lion, the Witch and the Wardrobe*. My mom and I read those books together when I was a kid."

"Did you know that C.S. Lewis was super-Christian, and that book is a religious allegory?"

"Well, my parents are dyed-in-the-wool atheists who taught me to mistrust religion at all costs."

"Not a bad idea," Zaylee says, sitting beside the dilapidated shed. "My parents are on the other side of the spectrum. We're not freaks, but we go to church every week. Not Catholic church, mind you. They chose Bishop for the quality of education."

I hunch down, plant myself beside her, splinters be damned, and pull my knees to my chest. "So, what is this secret spot?"

"I've never been able to figure that out," she says with a giggle that makes her sound younger. "It's like half-maintained, half-abandoned. Whatever, it's magical."

"It's cool." Wish I had something more profound to add.

Zaylee turns to face me, and I follow her lead. My heart's

thumping like a marching band drum, and the damp ground is soaking through my jeans. Are we about to kiss?

Suddenly, her face is closing in on mine at warp speed, and she licks my cheek. "Surprise," she whispers, then kisses me. Unlike Dana at Gilman, Zaylee tastes sweet, like rose petals and cherry cola. She places her hands on my cheeks and presses hard, opening her mouth wider and swirling her tongue around mine. This spot *is* magical.

"You don't kiss like a sophomore."

"Thank you." Then I lean in, and we begin kissing again. I'm having an out-of-body experience, like watching a love scene from *Romeo + Juliet*, that Claire Danes and Leonardo DiCaprio movie.

After a few minutes of exploring, catching breaths, and diving back in, Zaylee pats my back and gives me a much softer, formal peck on the cheek.

"OK, Zack," she says, standing up. "Let's get you home."

"Cool." Zaylee is definitely the boss here.

We reverse our route, exit the secret garden, part the bushes, hop the fence, and amble through the empty campus in a peaceful silence. I feel like what just happened is a sandcastle, and even a single word will wash it away.

As we cross the parking lot, Zaylee reaches over to take my hand. I can still taste her, but the essence is fading. I wish I could hold that flavor on my tongue, preserve it, and keep it as a souvenir.

Back in her Kia, Zaylee puts on a CD by Everclear and starts driving. The Saturday night lights of the East Bay shine from both sides of the freeway while the car zips along and the singer hollers about buying someone "a new life." That's what I feel is happening to me.

"So, Zack, why exactly are you friends with that guy?"

Boom. Back down to earth. "Who? Matthias?"

"Yes, *that* guy," she says. "Did I tell you he hangs outside the yogurt shop, skating and dancing alone? It's unnerving."

Pictures of Matthias in the pit at Gilman and behind the bleachers flash through my mind. "That's just Matthias being Matthias. He's harmless."

"Well, he's been trying to get my number for a long time. Not going to happen."

We don't speak for a while. Another Everclear song comes on; this one is called "Father of Mine," and the words are all about the singer's dad abandoning him. It cuts pretty close to the bone.

"How does it feel to be a senior?"

She turns the stereo down a notch. "Stressful. Everyone's applying to colleges, typical stuff."

"But, like, how does it *feel*?"

"Oh, you're a *sensitive* jock now. Since you asked, Zack, I can't wait to leave my parents' house. Their expectations can be exhausting."

"My mom makes me feel like that too."

"Well, you'll truly understand two years from now."

She laughs in a way that makes me feel young, but I don't mind. It's just awesome being here with her, in this warm car, with the music blaring and the world rushing by outside.

"Do you think I can get your number?" I ask when we pull up in front of my building.

"My number?" Zaylee locks eyes with me. "This," she says, pointing first at me, then herself, "was a one-time thing."

"I'm not like Matthias. I won't come by your store all the time and—"

Zaylee snorts. "I'm kidding, you nerd. Of course, you can have my number. You think I go around kissing sophomore polo players every weekend?" She pulls a pen out, grabs my wrist, and writes (510) 926-1023, adding plump hearts above both ones. "Use it," Zaylee says and drops my hand.

"Awesome." From the curb, I listen to the bass thump as the car takes off.

OK, forget the Gilman show. This was the best night of my life—unchallenged.

TWENTY
COVALENT BONDS

It's a drizzly mid-October afternoon, and Matthias and I are crowded in the rear of a bus heading towards Telegraph. I'm still dazzled by how self-sufficient these Berkeley kids are, hopping on buses everywhere, making their own plans. In Tempe, I was so sheltered.

"I'm not a moron, Dr. Z, but the class is impossible." Matthias's words are pouring out between agitated exhalations. "The way Mr. Katz teaches is so effing boring."

It's hard to follow his derailing thought train, but the gist is Matthias is convinced he's going to fail chemistry without immediate intervention.

"My mom says anyone who makes science boring should be tried for abuse."

He looks up, eyes glazed over. "What?"

"She's a science professor, so she's obsessed with the subject." That's a fact. In seventh grade, once we stayed up until midnight prepping for a test on atomic numbers and chemical symbols. "I'm not half bad at chem, Matty. I can help you study."

Matthias slaps his cheek so hard that his hand leaves a

pink mark. "For real? My parents tutored me through middle school, but that's where they tapped out."

"When's the test?"

"Day after tomorrow." He stands and pulls the thick bus cord. "Here's our stop."

We disembark, and as we walk, I take in the mingling scents of incense, marijuana, Indian food, and garbage. Berkeley isn't home yet, but it's getting closer—and Telegraph has claimed a piece of my heart.

Matthias is hopping on and off his skateboard, headphones blasting, barking "Hey!" along with the music. No one bats an eyelash. He's just another piece of the tapestry.

We pass a skate shop with clothes by DROORS, Santa Cruz, Acme, and a slew of other brands hanging in the window. The stuff looks righteous, and I wouldn't mind wearing some of it. Plenty of preppy kids wear skate clothes without knowing anything about skating. But I feel like I've borrowed enough from Matty; I can't bite his entire identity.

Matthias points across the street at the Slice of Life sign. "Screw the library. Let's study over some pizza." He jumps on his skate, which forces me to jog behind him.

We enter the pizza place, where Matthias's metalhead pal is behind the counter like he never left. "They're cracking down on freebies," he says, but still serves up a pair of pepperoni slices.

We slip into an open booth and set our greasy paper plates down. Matthias pulls out his textbook, and I open my backpack to get my copy. Despite the chasm between us in most subjects, we're somehow both taking chemistry this year.

"What chapter is your class up to?"

"Ionic versus covalent bonds," Matthias says, then proceeds to scarf down nearly half his slice in a single bite.

"Let's review for a sec." Mom helped me master this

concept, so I feel confident and somewhat superior. "The nonmetal attracts the electron. Atoms share electrons in their outer orbitals."

Matthias lets his head fall into his arms like an overgrown grade schooler. "I don't get this shit at all, man."

"Don't sweat it." I tap a diagram in his book. "We'll break it down into manageable chunks. Ionic bonds have high polarity, and covalent bonds have low."

A minute passes before Matthias lifts his head and brushes his hair from his eyes. Something changed. Now, there's a grin on his face. "Check it out," he says. "'I' rhymes with high, and 'co' rhymes with low. Ionic, high. Covalent, low." Matthias slaps the table so loud a guy eating by himself across the restaurant looks up. "I got this. Next one."

"Awesome, dude. So, ionic bonds are solid, and covalent bonds are liquids or gas."

Keeping my best tutor face on, I take a bite of pizza and wait.

"Well, I'm solid," he says, wiping some grease from around his mouth with the back of his hand. "So ionic, solid. I, solid."

"Works for me."

We continue like this for a while: Matthias finds ways to connect the dots between the facts with little tricks. He probably isn't gaining a deep understanding of the topics or how they relate to other facets of science, but at least he's got a shot at passing his test. And that's what we're here for.

"Matthias, you're getting this."

We keep going for twenty minutes without a break. Whenever we stop, Matthias delivers another demand: "Quiz me, Dr. Z!" Or just, "Again!"

The session turns out to be a bizarre success, but why would I expect anything else from Matty?

Finally, we spill onto the sidewalk on a post-study high and saunter to the bus stop.

We stand there in the fading fall light as cars zoom by. Matthias lights a cigarette and blows out a stream of smoke in the opposite direction from me.

"So," he says, with his back turned, "Noel saw you at the card shop near my house last weekend."

My breath catches in my sternum. *Noel, you little narc.* "Not many places have WWF cards. You know I like shit like that."

Matty takes a dramatic drag off his cig while giving me a smile like he knows I'm full of shit. "But you were waiting for that girl, Zaylee, right? Dude, I told you about her."

Yeah, right. You let me know you were into her and got dogged. What a nightmare. Why did Noel have to be in the mini-mall at the same time I was? And why didn't he make his presence known—say hi to his brother's friend or whatnot? Asshole maneuver.

"We hung out," I say casually. "She took me to her school." Keeping Zaylee a secret isn't possible, so I'll let him feel the sting of the truth.

"That girl *drove* you? In her car?"

"She's a senior." Now, I'm just showing off, like Zaylee said I do.

He takes another demonstrative puff, then drops his cigarette on the ground and grinds it with the heel of his Vans. "Nice one, Zack." Matthias raises his hand in expectation of a high five. "Older woman."

I give his palm a quick slap. "We talk on the phone a lot."

"Sounds like it's getting serious."

I can feel his jealousy. "Maybe. Here's our bus."

It's a quiet ride home with only a few other riders. Matthias puts his headphones on, closes his eyes, and sinks into himself, mouthing words along with his music. A few minutes later, he gets off to transfer. We don't say a word to each other, just nod goodbye.

I peer out my scratched-up window, watching the city go by, wondering what surprises Berkeley has in store for me next.

TWENTY-ONE
THE TEENAGE COMPENDIUM

Tonight, Mom has office hours for her students. She'll be home late, which gives me a chunk of alone time to pump some iron and call Zaylee. The thought makes me so ecstatic that I spontaneously shout "Yes!" so loudly that a runner across the street looks up.

Before heading inside, I pick up the mail from the common area. Typical junk: a stack of coupons and an AOL floppy disk in a plastic-covered mailer screaming "50 FREE Hours" and "It's Easy! It's Fun!" They're trying to get us on the internet from every angle.

Pushed far in the back is a manila envelope with a hand-written address, postmarked Santa Fe, New Mexico. Oh shit.

"Hey, Dad," I say involuntarily.

After rushing inside, I drop everything on the dining room table and stare at the envelope. My heart palpitates, and my stomach bubbles. What the hell does he want? And why can't he just use the phone like the rest of the world?

Mom explained to me how their split was amicable but that they agreed to give each other space. But in the two years since we last spoke, I haven't even gotten a postcard, and this letter is dredging up some nasty emotions.

I sit on the couch, slide my finger underneath the seal, and open the envelope like it contains secret documents. Inside is a tiny magazine, handwritten and stapled together. It has doodles all over it, and on the front, it says in messy letters, *The Teenage Compendium.*

Typical Dad. Bohemian to the bone.

The opening page reads, "The Hall of Fame," and from there, he's copied quotes from his favorite poets by hand.

> *Here are our thoughts - voyagers' thoughts,*
> *Here not the land, firm land, alone appears, may then by*
> *   them be said;*

— WALT WHITMAN

What can I say? Some parents played catch; my dad read to me from a hardcover copy of *Leave of Grass.*

> *So there sat they,*
> *The estranged two,*
> *Thrust in one pew*
> *By chance that day;*
> *Placed so, breath-nigh,*
> *Each comer unwitting*
> *Who was to be sitting*
> *In touch close by.*

— THOMAS HARDY

> *I meant to have but modest needs,*
> *Such as content, and heaven;*

Within my income these could lie,
And life and I keep even.

— EMILY ELIZABETH DICKINSON

Are he and I supposed to be the estranged two? Feels like it to me. More cryptic communications are crammed into every nook and cranny of the magazine. Finally, on the last page, is a message from Dad.

Dearest Zack,

I'll own up to the fact that I've been a coward and a runner. I doubt she's told you this, but I speak with your mother weekly. We were always close and remain so.

Before you were born, I wrote poems, stories, and essays. Then, with the responsibilities of parenthood, adulthood, and livelihood, I tossed that part of me in a drawer and closed it. Now, I'm living the life I left behind. What I've lost is our family. What I've gained is my muse and myself.

You are young. You're in the thick of it now. That will change. If there is one thing I know, it's that you have courage. Use it.

As for why I can't be with you now. I need to live, because I spent years just existing. Read this when you think of me and think of me when you read this. You probably won't forgive me, but I need you to understand me.

Love,
Dad

He talks to her every *week*. Is this a fucking joke? I walk outside and do ten reps, then run back inside to collapse on my bed. Mom's been feeding me the same line for the past two years: "Your father's a frustrated poet who is working on himself."

What a load of crap. She's still been in contact with the guy.

This letter—this hippy art magazine he sent me, whatever it is—represents a betrayal of epic proportions. And I'm gonna call her on it. But first, I dial Zaylee's number, which I have memorized. The phone cools the side of my face, and the ringtone is a soothing beep, unlike the Arizona one, which seems rowdy in my memory.

When she answers, I can hardly keep myself from jumping into the Dad stuff. *Keep things light, Coleman. Don't scare her off.* "How was school?" I ask.

"Incredibly boring. But I turned in an English paper that's been driving me batshit," Zaylee says in a fake upper-crust voice.

"What's it about?"

"It's a comparison of two poets: Walt Whitman and Dylan Thomas."

Hearing Zaylee mention Walt Whitman is too much of a coincidence. I break down and vomit everything onto her: my parent's divorce, *The Teenage Compendium*, my need to confront my mom about their secret chats. When I'm done, I expect Zaylee to hang up the phone, say "Whatever," and never want to talk to me again.

She inhales deeply. "Well, there's more to you than I thought, young grasshopper."

"Because of my problems with my Dad?"

"Because you got real with me, and I like that."

I feel my neck flush. "It helps that you're a great listener."

"Go talk to your Mom, you nerd. Sounds like you two have some stuff to work out."

Zaylee's encouragement was exactly what I needed. Half an hour later, when Mom walks through the door, I'm ready to go head-to-head in a cage match of honesty.

"Guess who wrote me a letter?" I whip *The Teenage Compendium* and letter from behind my back and slap them against my open palm.

Mom stops in her tracks; my surprise attack worked.

She takes the envelope and magazine from me and scrunches her eyes to inspect the evidence. "From the looks of the address, I'm going with your father? He said he might do something like that."

We just entered the ring, and she's already fessed up. This is too easy. "Mom, how can you be so chill about keeping a secret like you two talking?"

"Parents aren't obligated to share every detail with their kids. I hoped it wouldn't become an issue."

"It's a big fucking issue. You get human contact while I get poetry and doodles."

"I think your father is reaching out in his own creative way," Mom says while flipping through the pages. "Silas wants to share his love of language with you."

My throat clenches up, and warm tears pour down my cheeks. I feel like running out of the room, kicking a hole in the wall, anything but crying. "It's not the letter," I say. "It's that you're still talking to him, and no one seems to think that's slightly weird at all. He's my dad, for God's sake."

Mom walks over and wraps her arms around me. How did I go from my epic truth takedown to sniffling into my mother's shoulder?

"Silas will wisen up and re-engage with you," she says. "As for us staying in touch, that's something I need to do for me. It's hard to let people go, even after they disappoint you."

"But what do you two even talk about?"

"Things happening in our lives. Adult stuff—our business."

"Whatever." I break the hug and reach out my hand. "Can I have those back, please?"

Mom places Dad's magazine on the kitchen table where it sits, like a dare, until I grab it and stuff it under my arm.

"Since we're talking honestly, Zack, how are things?"

She's broken me down. "I met a girl. She's a senior."

"Taking after your mother. Don't forget Silas is younger than me by two years."

Yuck. I try unsuccessfully to purge my mind of Dad and Mom smooching in the '70s. "Her name is Zaylee. She attends a private Catholic school and is brilliant and politically involved."

"Zack, if she likes you, I already know she's a good person."

I can feel the waterworks starting again, but I force my mouth down and scrunch my forehead to hold the tears back. "Just do me a favor. Let Dad know I want to talk to him," I say. "Tell him I'm mature enough."

"Honey, you were *always* mature enough. God knows you were the most grown-up of the three of us."

My stone-faced pose crumbles, and I smile because that is so obviously true.

TWENTY-TWO
COMPANY WE KEEP

It's been a grueling morning practice, and I'm toweling off in the locker room when Coach Reardon approaches me. He hardly ever comes into the players' area, so as soon as I see him stride over, I know something's up.

"Coleman," he says without meeting my eye. "You got five minutes before homeroom? I want to talk to you." I must look concerned because Reardon quickly follows up with, "I'll write you a note."

"Be right there," I say while shoving my Old Spice stick up the front of my shirt, rubbing under one arm, then the other. I tug my shoes on and sling my backpack over my shoulder. You don't keep the coach waiting.

My stomach turns as I approach his office. I'm not used to getting a talking-to. I thought our last practice went well —I even assisted a couple of critical shots.

"Take a seat." Reardon leans back in his chair, hands behind his neck. "Here's the deal, Zack."

He never calls us by our first names—a bad sign.

"I've been impressed with your playing, sportsmanship, and flexibility."

"Thank you, Coach."

"I don't make it my business to investigate what every player does with their free time," he continues.

While Reardon stares at the ceiling, I count the leathery rings of skin on his neck. It's a futile challenge—the guy is ancient.

"But with that in mind." He coughs. "I've been keeping an eye on you, seeing as you're new and all."

The image of my high school water polo coach spying on me in the halls is sinister as hell, but I'm smart enough to know when to suck up to an authority figure. "Appreciate that, Coach."

He taps his desk a few times. "I have to tell you, Zack, I'm not too pleased with your choice of friends." The old man levels his stare at me, forcing our eyes to meet. "Those skateboard kids are bad news."

"Bad news?" I can hardly believe how disrespectful I sound. "Those skateboard kids are my friends."

"That one friend of yours..." Reardon catches my eye, so I know precisely who he means. "He's got charisma, maybe even some skill at whatever it is he does—"

"Skating."

"Sure, *skating*." He lays into the second word like it stole his prom date. "Riding skateboards is a fun pastime. What you do in the water requires real discipline."

In the silence that follows, it seems like he expects me to say something, but all I want is to leave this shitty office and return to my life. "I get it, Coach."

He narrows his eyes in their weather-beaten sockets. "Course you do." He offers his best attempt at a smile. "It's just that in life, we have opportunities, right? The people you surround yourself with now can impact your future."

He interlocks his fingers and leans forward. "You're

going places. Those kids aren't. I can tell you in a hundred ways, but you know what I mean."

Reardon is close enough that I can smell his coffee breath. I sink my nails into the tops of my legs. "Yes, Coach."

"Remember, we are the company we keep."

Somehow, I keep myself composed after our chat and make my way to homeroom, where, in his classic stoned way, Danny Chang shuffles over and asks if I'm OK. He's a good dude, but I shake my head, unable to find words to explain why I'm so furious.

I can't concentrate during my morning classes. My mind and nervous system are conspiring to create turbulent internal weather. I'm taking hits from all sides: Mom betrays me by talking to Dad, Dad sends poetic riddles instead of calling, and Reardon spies on me at school. And Matthias—what is this hold he has on me?

Zaylee is a bright spot, a swath of blue sky poking through the storm clouds in my head. I feel most like myself when we're talking. But even then, I'm constantly double-checking what I say to sound older. Plus, she keeps telling me her family is full-on into church, and we've always been non-religious.

Lunch hits, and I head back to the bleachers like I'm on autopilot. I see Rob, Tina, Matthias, and a few freshmen in baggy skater gear I recognize from the park. With my head full of Reardon, they look like a bunch of hooligans to me. His speech from this morning echoes in my mind: "You're going places. Those kids aren't."

Maybe the old man is right. Could I be selling myself short?

Matthias sees me and skates over, punching me hard in the shoulder when we meet. "Look," he says, holding up his arm. In his fist is a piece of paper with a red Sharpied C+.

"For an emaciated person, you're damn strong," I say, rubbing the spot where he socked me. "How'd you get that test back that fast?"

Matthias folds the test and slips it carefully into his back pocket. "Peer grading. Mr. Katz is way into it. Instant gratification, bro."

Now, I'm the one offering my hand up for a high five. "Matthias, that's awesome. Seriously, I'm proud of you, dude."

"Couldn't have done it without you, buddy." Matthias brings his head to my ear. "Guess what?" he whispers, though the others are out of earshot. "I got us something to celebrate with."

Hopefully, that doesn't mean more stolen CDs. "What?"

He smiles, bares his teeth, and does a punk rock jig around his board. "It's a surprise."

I follow Matthias as he skates back to Rob, Tina, and the grommets. "I'm not great with surprises."

Matthias looks back at me from his board. "Don't worry, Dr. Z. You're gonna trip. Literally."

"So, should I meet you at your place?"

"No, sir," he says with a far-off look in his eyes. "Saturday, I'm coming to Casa de Zachariah. It's time to see how the other half lives."

I've unwittingly bought a ticket for another flight to an unknown destination.

After lunch is world history, which is a guaranteed snoozefest. Mr. Sylvain is one of those teachers who does everything he can to make the class enjoyable: talks in voices, pretends to be characters from history, swears to prove he's hip, and shows us movies like *History of the World, Part I* and *Bill & Ted's Excellent Adventure*. He's a good teacher—he doesn't grade hard and lets you take a test over if you bomb. But the material is tedious.

"After Constantinople was taken over by the Ottoman Turks in 1453, Sultan Mehmed II took a new title." Mr. Sylvain drones on and on. "And this is interesting. See, the name he chose was Kayser-i Rûm. That's like Turkish for Caesar of Rome." He pauses. "You can hear it, right?"

No matter how hard Mr. Sylvain works to inject some personality into his lessons, comparing life under Russian and Byzantine Rulers will always be dry.

On top of this insufferable lecture, there's the added intensity of Matthias coming to my house over the weekend with a "surprise." It's too much to think about, so I distract myself by daydreaming about Zaylee. I imagine her driving us around Berkeley and crossing the Bay Bridge into San Francisco. We go to Fisherman's Wharf and walk around holding hands and kissing in public, like in a movie. Later, we go out to eat at a fancy restaurant—my treat—and laugh and spoon dessert into each other's mouths.

"So, Zack," Mr. Sylvain asks, interrupting the romantic machinations of my imagination. "Why exactly do we consider the Byzantines the 'preservers of classical knowledge'?"

My fantasy date evaporates. "That's an excellent question." I hustle and search the dense paragraphs.

"It is an excellent question," replies Mr. Sylvain. "That's why I asked." Some kids snicker.

So, what you have to know is that the Byzantines did a lot of…" The answer is in the caption beneath a photo of a monk. "Copying and transcribing. That's it, copying and transcribing."

Mr. Sylvain gives me a golf clap. "Nice save, Zack."

Even though he's being sarcastic, I appreciate his vote of confidence. Now let's see if I can try some heroics and keep the rest of my life from falling apart.

TWENTY-THREE
POETICS

"You've got a Friday night date, and the phone is ringing off the hook. What are you, a teenager or something?"

"Whatever," I say and glare at my mom.

We're just finishing dinner and Zaylee will be here any minute to pick me up, so I'm hella jumpy. Mom's right, though. Lately, the phone *is* always for me. Right now, the shrill repetition of the ring sends a current of electricity through my body —a Pavlovian reaction like we learned about in middle school.

"Hey, Desert Rat."

"What's up, man?"

"Look, Dr. Z, we're tight, right? Like blood brothers?" Matty sounds downright frantic.

"Sure, I guess."

"See, I've been thinking about all kinds of things—skating, the universe, music, existence itself. And I've decided we need to trip together," he declares.

Trip? He used that word at school. I cradle the phone to my neck and walk out of earshot. "Not sure what you mean." But I fear I do.

"What I mean is that ordinary morality is for ordinary people."

These don't sound like the words of my almost-failing-chemistry buddy. Lately, Matthias is never the same person two days in a row. "Where'd you hear that?"

He lets out a long, horror-movie cackle. "The mysterious, mystical magician Aleister Crowley."

"Crow-who?" Always some new obscure reference.

"The occult genius."

"OK, that's not weird at all."

He must sense my hesitation because he changes the subject. "Tomorrow night, we kick it. Or are you tied up with that girl?"

Matty must be psychic—Zaylee is on her way over this second. But I'm smart enough to avoid saying anything about her. "Nah, Saturday's cool."

"Invite your friend over," Mom says too loudly as she takes the pizza box into the kitchen.

"My mom is psyched to meet you," I say, though the thought of them in the same room fills me with terror. Their energy fields will cancel each other out.

"You've seen my world. Now I'm gonna see yours." Matthias takes a deep breath, like he's going scuba diving. "This weekend, you and I are gonna become blood brothers."

Occult geniuses, blood brothers—time to cut out. "Look, I have to help my mom clean up, or she'll be pissed. See you tomorrow."

"Later, Dr. Z."

"You alright, hon?" Mom looks at me with a hand on her hip and a wrinkled forehead.

"Just tired or whatever." It's like she can tell how tense that conversation made me. Is everyone a mind reader?

"Have you heard how certain people can take your power away?"

I pick up our plates and walk them to the sink. "No, Mom, I haven't."

"Well, they can." She spins me around by the shoulder, so we're eye to eye. "And when they do, it's up to you to take that power back."

Right on time, the doorbell rings, and Mom's head turns like it's a long-awaited shipment of lab supplies. Looks like this is going to be a weekend of awkward firsts. Why not rip the Band-Aid off and let Mom meet my hopefully-soon-to-be girlfriend?

I open the door to find Zaylee leaning against the porch wall in a jean skirt over leggings and a cool bomber jacket covered with pins. She's wearing her hair up in two little twists with a bunch of barrettes at different angles. She looks incredibly cool without trying too hard. I wish I could learn that trick.

"Hey," she says.

"Hey."

"I'm Margaret." Mom extends a bangled wrist past me. "It's so nice to meet you, Zaylee. Zack's been raving about you but neglected to mention how utterly lovely you are."

This is mortifying. "How exactly would I mention that Mom?"

Zaylee laughs in that effortless way of hers, as if nothing's that big a deal because the world has so many more significant problems. "No worries, Zack. Everyone knows you can't stop talking about me."

Soon, the two of them start gushing over one another's outfits, yakking it up, with me standing like a dummy on the sidelines. It hits me: these are two grown women talking. Zaylee could even be my mom's student next year.

That revelation sends me down a rapid spiral of future

tripping: Zaylee goes to college, and my life consists of Matthias, skaters, water polo idiots, and Coach Reardon. "We'd better go," I say, brushing away nightmares of high school purgatory.

"Nice to meet you, Mrs. Coleman." Zaylee is truly the poster child for Catholic school politeness.

"Maggie." Mom gives her a half-hug.

The shortened version of my mom's name is a serious gold star. I can't recall anyone but Dad calling her that, and that was only when they were in a fight.

Minutes later, Zaylee is speeding us through Berkeley, blasting Gin Blossoms as the city lights smear to the sound-track of chiming chords and the singer's fluttery, forlorn voice.

With the windows rolled down and evening air slapping my cheeks, my stress evaporates. Screw Dad's letter, Matthias's tripped-out talk, and Reardon's warning. I'm alive and free.

Zaylee taps on the steering wheel, adorably out of rhythm. "I freakin' love this band."

"This song is awesome." I can't stop staring at her half-lit profile.

"What are you looking at?"

I've seen enough movies to know the correct response. "You look gorgeous."

She pats my knee. "You still want to go to the movies?"

"Do you?"

Zaylee smiles, turns up the music, and takes the next freeway exit. We pass through a few intersections of strip malls and gas stations.

"You are now entering the swanky part of Oakland. Welcome to beautiful Rockridge." Zaylee turns down a quiet, leafy street and settles on a dark place to park. She shuts the engine off.

"So, does this mean we're skipping the movie?"

"Guess so," Zaylee says, unfastening her seatbelt and leaning so close I can smell the peach essence of her shampoo. She kisses me softly on the mouth, but it's a fake-out. Soon, she's got her hands on the back of my head, and we're full-on making out, her mouth opening wide, tongue licking the front of my teeth.

She tastes like cinnamon, and when my eyes open, I notice a pack of Big Red on the dashboard. That annoying gum commercial song passes through my head.

"Wait a minute," she says, reaching over my stomach to ease my seat back so I'm reclining. She starts rubbing against me—not like Dana at Gilman—more like a cat.

Zaylee takes my right hand and puts it up her shirt against her warm belly. Then she places my palm on her bra, which is silkier and looser than I would have guessed. Unsure of what to do next, I rub my hand in circles while she makes purring sounds.

Here's the thing. It's not like I haven't fantasized about this happening, but she's moving so fast I can barely keep up. Older women don't waste time. A few more hot and heavy minutes later, Zaylee pulls away and fixes her hair.

What do I say? "You're an amazing kisser."

"Likewise. Not bad for a sophomore."

My seat suddenly springs back up loudly.

"Smooth," Zaylee says.

"That's my middle name."

"So, what is it about him?"

"Who?" I reply, but we both know who she's talking about. Why is everyone so concerned about me and Matty lately?

"That guy. Matthias or whoever."

"He's the first true friend I made here. Well, except for this guy, Danny."

She fixes her twists in the rearview mirror. "You two are nothing alike."

"Maybe opposites attract or something. Matty is super-knowledgeable about a lot of stuff. Underground music, skating."

"What about politics or social issues?" she inquires. "You get a pass, since you just moved to Berkeley, but we'll get you involved soon enough."

The Save the Coast button on Zaylee's sweater glares at me, daring me to recall when Matthias or I took a stand on an issue. "Matty told me about Harvey Milk and a bunch of the bands he introduced me to are super political. Like Dead Kennedys, Propaghandi—"

"Harvey Milk is an important Bay Area figure for sure. But Propaghandi? That can't be a real band name."

"It is, and they're super rad." I reach over and smooth Zaylee's hair. She responds by resting her head on my shoulder.

"Well, if you see something in him, he could be all right."

A car turns down the street, illuminating the interior of Zaylee's car: some scratched-up CDs on the floor, three empty packs of Big Red, and a pamphlet that reads *On Berkeley Soil: California's Groundwater Deregulation Brownfield Containment Policy.*

"That doesn't look like light reading," I say, half-joking.

"It isn't a light issue."

When Zaylee drops me off, I find Mom on the couch, papers spread everywhere, so I can see she's been working, not waiting up for me. Yeah, right. There's no chance of slipping by unnoticed.

"Zaylee is lovely. Not that I'm surprised; you're a catch yourself."

Maybe there's an upside to Dad missing out on my formative teenage years; he isn't around for these excruciating play-by-plays of my dating life. "Yeah, she's pretty awesome."

Mom sits up, looking all giddy. "What did you two do?"

My mind flashes to us making out, my hands beneath Zaylee's top. The image makes me involuntarily cough. "We went to the new Jim Carrey movie, and Zaylee dropped me off after. It was chill."

Mom makes a "hmm" sound and crosses her legs. "Well," she begins tentatively. "I'm glad you introduced me to Zaylee, and it'll be great to meet Matthias too."

"Can't wait." But I'd like to wait a long time. Like forever.

TWENTY-FOUR
BLOOD BROTHERS

All day Saturday, everything feels unfocused and out of control. A leaf blower creates an unbelievable racket outside, making lifting weights or reading impossible. Mom is cleaning up inside while howling along with that song, "What if God Was One of Us?" Yup, it's that kind of morning.

It's an odd feeling knowing Matthias will be in *my* house. Compared to his close-knit clan, Mom and I seem more like roommates. Finally, the doorbell rings. I slide across the living room in my socks and fling the front door open.

"Yo, my blood brother."

That phrase is officially beginning to freak me out. "Hey, Matty."

He follows me into the living room, where Mom appears in a sparkly top, heels, and makeup.

"Hello, Mrs. Coleman," Matthias says, hunching both shoulders. "It's cool to meet Dr. Z's mother."

"Well, I've heard a lot about you, Matthias," she replies coolly. Unlike her instant rapport with Zaylee, there's no first name tonight. "Zack says you are a very talented skate-boarder."

Matthias looks up. "That's cool. Yeah, I like to skate."

"He's being modest, Mom. Matty is incredible."

She attempts to catch Matthias's eyes, which are shielded by bangs. I can't imagine what he looks like to her—drowning in his jeans, frayed bottoms trailing behind bulky sneakers.

"Well, Zack is a superb athlete. Wrestling, water polo, any sport, really."

"That's the truth. Dr. Z is a machine."

Mom click-clacks across the floor. The sound reminds me of her and Dad attending university functions and leaving me at home with a sitter.

"I'll be out with Geoff this evening." She lightly touches both sides of her hair, urging it to stay in place. "There's left-over pizza. You have money if you need anything else."

"We're going to stick around here," I say. "Walk around the neighborhood, go to the park or wherever."

Having someone new in our apartment magnifies every detail: insanely tidy bookshelves, over-swept floors, spotless walls, and Z Gallerie prints. Our single-mother-and-kid setup is a galaxy far, far away from his family's warm, messy home. We head to my bedroom.

"Dude," he says, looking over my posters and trophy shelf. "I had no idea how into wrestling you were."

"The Undertaker and Kane are pretty punk rock if you ask me."

"I'm only playing, man," he says. "Noel and I watch WWF. He loves it. I have to keep reminding him it's fake."

Matthias takes a spot on the floor and pulls his legs up to his chest. His back is so bony the outline of his spine shows through his shirt. "Your house is chill, Dr. Z. I can hear my wheels turning here."

The screen door slams, and I hear Mom laugh at something. Geoff must be outside. "Have a good night, boys," she calls out.

"Your mom seems dope," Matthias says

"She can be uptight about weird things, but I guess she's cool."

I put on A Tribe Called Quest and sit on the floor with my back against the bed. The beats fill the room, softening the air molecules. Honestly, Matthias stealing this CD for me seems like eons ago. Those were simpler times, before Zaylee, before my doubts about him.

Matthias bobs his head, hair spilling over his face. "This album is pure magic. And tonight will be magic too." His giggling blends with the music; it sounds almost sinister.

Suddenly, Matty springs up and starts doing herky-jerky moves in front of my closet mirror.

"You want to see the neighborhood? It's boringsville, but we've got a decent park."

"Sure, man. But first…" Matthias pulls a crinkled plastic bag from deep in the front pocket of his jeans and flattens it on the floor. Stuck to the sides of the baggie are broken stems and flecks of brown leaf around what look like dried-up cow patties.

I'm no drug expert, but the parking lot hippies at my high school in Tempe taught me a couple of things. "Shrooms?"

"That's right. Silly psilocybin. One of Albert Hofmann's killer inventions."

"Who?"

"Same dude who discovered LSD, my blood brother." He laughs maniacally, making me wonder if he's already taken some. "See, I know some science too."

"Apparently." Drugs scare the shit out of me. There are a million horror stories about kids taking mushrooms and acid and losing their minds. Talking to lampposts, ending up homeless—dire scenarios. Plus, coaches pound you with anti-drug talk. Keeping high school sports teams relatively sober is how you win championships.

"I promised you something for helping me pass that test." Matthias shakes two large specimens from the bag and displays them in his palm.

"Matty, I have a game this week."

"Bro." Matthias leans in and pushes his hair back, revealing bloodshot eyes, a cluster of small pimples around his hairline, and at least four or five light white scars that look skateboard-related. "Everyone is scared the first time they trip."

For good reason.

He pulls a Snickers bar from his pocket and rips the wrapper with his teeth. "This will help because caps taste like ass." He chomps down on the side of the candy bar and pops both shrooms in his mouth.

Matthias begins to chew loudly, and a lengthy string of Snickers descends from his mouth. Finally, he swallows and grins.

"You don't have to take caps that big." Matthias shakes the bag and hands me a few twigs. "Try these stems."

All the air suddenly feels like it's been sucked from the room. Before I can dissuade myself, I grab what's left of the candy bar, toss the twigs into my mouth, and chase them down with a generous chunk of Snickers.

Then I chew like I've never chewed before.

Whenever the mushroom flavor cuts through the choco-late-peanut defense shield, I chomp down harder.

"A Deadhead told me that they grow these things in cow dung," I say out the side of my mouth. "Hope that's an urban legend."

From far away, Matthias's voice says. "Keep chewing.

Mash it all up. You need to get it all digested. Trust me, I've been doing this since sixth grade."

The words reverberate. Sixth grade…sixth grade…sixth grade.

"Let's go to that park, Dr. Z."

So we float out of the house and onto the street. Am I feeling anything? At first, I think I do. Then I'm sure it's my imagination. Wait, did we close the door behind us?

"Matthias?" My voice is ultra-quiet. I feel as if my ears are full of cotton. "Is the door locked?" I dash back to the house to find it bolted.

"You're tripping," Matthias says, laughing as we roll down the sidewalk. He's humming a song, and now it's in my head, too. Did he send the music to me? A tingling sensation fills my chest. The sunset looks beautiful.

"Matty, do you think I'm tripping?"

"Maybe a little," he replies. "But this is just the beginning. Relax and hang tight with me."

We make it down to the corner and wait through three rounds of stoplights. The first two don't feel right; the third time is the charm, so we cross.

Now, we're walking around the park. Is it Saturday night? The answer eludes me. Where is Mom again? Oh, on her date with bearded Geoff. He seems like a kind person. I realize I love her and want her to be happy.

We sit our asses on the grass across from two young kids playing soccer with their parents. They make easy goals and squeal with delight. "Hey, Matthias." I punch him in the arm. "Is that shit adorable or what?"

"Hella." Matthias lies down on the grass.

His eyes are closed, and his hair falls away from his forehead. I imagine it sliding off his head like a wig. "Hey, are you tripping?"

"A little," Matty answers. "Why are you whispering?"

Have I been whispering? "I think I might be tripping," I say louder.

"Dr. Z, you don't need to blast the whole park with that information. There are little kids. Let's hit those swings over there." Matthias points at the playground.

We walk over, and each of us claims a swing. I push my feet against the ground, step backward through the crunchy tanbark, and let go. Now, I'm hoisting myself into the air, maximizing my momentum, and it feels incredible.

"Why did we ever stop swinging after grade school?" I yell to the heavens.

I keep on swinging and never want to stop. The bars are shaking, and Matthias is cackling like the Wicked Witch of the West next to me. My heart is humming, and my eyes feel fuzzy. Soon, I'm scared I'll flip over the top of the swing set. I let my legs flop beneath me. "I need to…slow down."

Matty is so high now he disappears into the sky each time he ascends. I call out to him, "You have to come down!"

When I finally stop, my butt is molded to the seat. I hang my head and peer at my palms, which stare up from my lap like twin maps. For a split second, I find Tempe, but it vanishes.

Now that I know what drugs are like, I can't understand why society works so hard to keep them from us. A ghost version of Coach Reardon appears before me, wagging his cane in my direction. Poof—I brush him away with my powerful map hands. *Get out of my trip.*

How long have I been on the swing with my eyes closed, thinking? I picture Zaylee and want—no, need—to call her. There's too much to tell her about how I'm unlocking my mind.

Synapses are firing, giving me fresh insights: Mom needs

companionship, and Dad needs to believe he's an artist. What do I need? To win? Be accepted?

"What do you need?" Did I speak that aloud or think it?

I turn to the red leather swing seat next to me, but it's vacant. Instead of swinging, Matthias is staggering around the playground, lost in free-form contortions. "Hey." I stand up, then slump back down into my swing seat. "Matty, what do you need?"

Matthias turns, eyes shining. "I need love. We all do."

I wobble like one of those inflatable tube man dancers that advertise furniture sales and place an arm on each of Matthias's shoulders. He's sweaty and stinks. I pull him close.

"I'll never forget how you accepted me when I was new here."

He hugs me back. "No big deal, Dr. Z. We're two of a kind on the inside. I could tell when Danny Chang introduced us."

Danny. My heart beams with immeasurable gratitude for that stoner and the friendship he brought me. The night is getting chilly, and I'm still holding Matthias tight. We can see directly into each other's souls; there's no reason to hide anything. "But I can't even skate."

"Dude, you're my best friend." Matthias hugs me tighter.

"You're mine." At the sound of a far-off siren, I break the embrace. "Should we walk to my house? I can't remember, but I might need to be somewhere."

"Let's head back. We can eat and chill out."

The thought of eating makes me notice my belly twisting and turning. "Is it normal for my stomach to hurt so bad?"

Matthias wipes his neck down with the back of his shirt.

"That's your body trying to get rid of the shrooms. They're poison, but good poison. That's why they give you visions."

Poison? Visions? I shove the thoughts aside. Somehow, we arrive at the apartment in one piece. Mom's still out. As promised, there's a box of pizza in the refrigerator. Five slices left. Perfect.

Matthias inspects the inside of the fridge. "It's so clean."

"My mom's a stickler. She hates a mess."

In my room, I put on Bad Religion, but press stop after the first few seconds. "The guitar is slicing into me," I say. We burst into simultaneous laughter.

"Play Tribe again," Matthias commands from the bed. He's lying on his back, looking at the ceiling like he's Peter Pan thinking about flying across the night sky. "That album is perfection," he says.

He's right. Those beats, voices, and disembodied sounds are the ideal soundtrack for our trip. When the CD finishes, Matthias doesn't even open his eyes. "Again."

I stand, press play, and we get transported to another galaxy once more. This time, the album finishes in what feels like minutes.

"Again," Matthias says with a laugh.

I do as he commands. Without realizing it, I'm moving to the music. And before I know it, I'm dancing, grooving in my own way, swaying loose and slow beside Matty as he throws air punches.

From a faraway land on the other side of the door comes a voice. "Zack, I'm home. Does Matthias need a ride?"

A tsunami of dread invades our shroomy kingdom.

"Dude, we cannot let her see us like this, and there's no way she's driving you home. What the hell are we going to do?"

Matthias puts both hands on my shoulders. "Take a breath, Dr. Z. I'll sleep over. My parents won't care." His words work like a spell, dissolving my fear.

"Mom," I yell. "Matthias is gonna stay over." I search for

a detail—so everything seems normal. The crumb-filled cardboard box calls to me. "We finished the pizza like you said we should."

"Fine, I'm going to bed." Even through my mushroom haze, I can tell she's been drinking. It's a tone I remember from Tempe—nights when she and Dad returned home talking loudly, arguing about nature versus nurture or something.

"Hey, man, what's up?" Matthias noticed my mood change; that's how psychically bonded we are now.

"Just thinking about my Dad. Look at this magazine he made me." I take *The Teenage Compendium* off my desk and show it to Matty.

He flips through the pages and examines the magazine from every angle, paying particular attention to the drawings. "Wow, looks like your pops really did do some tripping in his time."

"That's just the way his brain works," I explain. "I'm starting to feel more normal. I think the shrooms are fading."

We're both sitting on the floor now, and Matty rests his head on my bed. "Yeah, I'm coming down a bit too. You wanna know the first time I took acid?"

"Tell me."

"In sixth grade."

"Where the hell does a kid that young get acid?"

"Where do you think? At the skatepark. High school kids thought it was funny to get me high." Matthias rubs his hand over his face. "I outshredded them all—even in sixth grade. I was a badass young skater."

"I was a badass young wrestler."

"We're two of a kind, Dr. Z." He yawns. "You got a blanket or a sleeping bag or something?"

I slip out of my jeans and into my gym shorts. It feels

safe to venture outside the fort, so I tiptoe into the hall and take a couple pillows and an old patchwork quilt from the closet.

"Here you go." I toss the bedding in Matthias's direction. "You can have the living room couch if you want."

"Is it cool if I take the opposite side of your bed?" Matthias is already pulling the quilt over him

"Of course, man."

I climb under the covers. I'm not used to having another person in my bed, and it's too toasty for my taste. Matthias may be gaunt, but the guy sure gives off a lot of heat. It's hard to find a comfortable position, but the day is catching up with me, and soon my head feels like a hundred-pound weight. As I drift off, I hear Matty repeating two words to himself: "blood brothers."

TWENTY-FIVE
AFTERMATH

I wake up in the morning in soaked sheets with both of my eyes blinking uncontrollably. "What are these yellow and red circles I'm seeing?"

"Tracers." Matthias is on the floor studying the rug like it's a treasure map.

"Do they ever go away?'

"Sure, bro. I only see them sometimes." He looks at me and raises an eyebrow. "Just kidding."

"Jesus, I hope my mind doesn't turn into mush from taking shrooms once."

"You're a brainiac, Dr. Z. You'll be fine."

We stagger into the kitchen like a pair of miners emerging from an underground cave.

Matthias seats himself at the kitchen island, where he looks completely chill. His laid-back skater demeanor is the perfect cover-up for being high. I hope I can pull off a lucid conversation with this technicolor tracer sideshow distracting me.

Luckily, Mom is moving pretty slowly this morning. Guess we all had a memorable night.

"I can't tell you boys how nice it was to get out with Geoff last night," she says, pouring coffee into a cactus-shaped mug. "I've been locked in a classroom or office hours for weeks."

Things must be getting serious with Geoff since she keeps pseudo-casually dropping his name.

"Sounds fun, Mom." I shake some corn flakes into my bowl.

"Teachers have to cut loose, too," Matthias pipes in.

"Correct. *Professors* are people too."

I know for a fact it drives her nuts when people call her a teacher.

"Seems like you were home early," she says. "What mischief did you two get up to?"

My heart stops; she's onto us. But Mom only takes a slow sip of coffee and turns from me to Matthias with genuine, innocent interest. Margaret Coleman has no idea about our psychedelic excursion. Like none. Phew.

"We took a trip," Matthias begins, without looking up from his cereal, "to the park."

I kick him under the table. "Just a mellow Saturday night. Walked around. Came home and listened to music."

"Lovely."

"So, what about you and Geoff?" I inquire, anxious to change the subject.

Mom gets a faraway look in her eyes. "Little of this, little of that. There may have been margaritas involved."

"Too much information, Mom," I say, striving to sound normal. For a second, she has a slight rainbow aura. Am I still tripping?

"Go, Mrs. Coleman," says Matthias. "Can I have some more orange juice?"

"Yes, you certainly *may*."

We eat and sip in silence. Thank God.

Matthias pushes his bowl away. "Gotta head out soon. I promised Noel a skating sesh. Thanks for breakfast, Mrs. Coleman."

We head back to my room, where it's safe and I don't have to keep my brain together in front of my mother.

"Take it easy, Dr. Z," Matty says as he collects his backpack from my floor. "Remember, the day after tripping is for laying low, soaking up all the insights."

I walk him to the front door and watch Matty slink across the courtyard. A few sunrays poke through the marine layer, creating shadows resembling spears on the ground. Or it could be my half-hallucinating brain.

After showering, I take a jog in the neighborhood. Sweat coats my forehead and neck faster than usual. On the right, I pass by the playground where Matty and I sat on the swing set. Everything looks different today, shimmery and extra bright.

As I run, I feel a fuzzy warmth throughout my body, like my skin possesses an extra layer, a sensory memory of the mushrooms. A wave of regret hits me—for keeping something from Mom and betraying Coach Reardon and the team. This must be the comedown Matthias was talking about.

I need to tell Zaylee what I did last night. It's imperative.

After crashing through the screen door, I scoop the phone off the floor and drag it into my room. An older woman's voice answers.

"Can I speak with Zaylee? This is Zack." *Do I sound high?*

"Zack?" The woman says my name like she's never heard it in her life. "Honey," she calls in a singsong voice. "Someone named Zack is on the phone for you."

"Hey," Zaylee says. Her mother hangs up, and we're alone on the line. "I didn't hear from you yesterday."

"I'm sorry. Things got pretty weird. What did you do?"

"Not much. Went to a movie with my parents—*Seven Years in Tibet*."

"How was that?"

She laughs. "Long and slow, but I won't complain about a few hours in a theater looking at Brad Pitt."

"Wish I could have come with you guys, but I guess you're still keeping me a secret from your family."

"Zack, give it a rest. We'll get there."

"So you say." I want to talk more about us. Unfortunately, a gripping compulsion to spill my guts stands in the way. "So," I say, holding the word way too long, "I took mushrooms last night."

"You mean, you took *drugs*?"

"Well, mushrooms aren't drugs exactly. They're natural, for cleansing your mind."

"Are you on drugs now?" Zaylee whispers.

"No, it's not like that. This was last night." But, actually, I wonder if I am still a bit altered.

She sighs. "Let me guess—Matthias."

"Yes, but I only took a little. Shrooms are less of a big deal than people make them out to be. I mean, they're from the earth." That's a lie—it was life-changing. But that won't win me any brownie points right now.

"You don't have to do everything that guy does. He's bad news."

"You don't know him that well," I say. "He's a unique person."

"I know plenty," Zaylee says, her voice softening. "For instance, I know you're a million times more unique than him."

"How so?"

"You know about Dylan Thomas and Walt Whitman, which immediately puts you on a different intellectual level than most high school jocks."

"I believe that's what they call a backhanded compliment."

"Oh?"

"Athletics and academics aren't mutually exclusive."

"I know that, you dummy," Zaylee says, exasperation seeping out like air from a deflating bicycle tire. "I mean, you're not a Richie-Rich kid, and you're not a jock. You're just Zack from Arizona."

"Thanks, I think."

"Also, you appreciate my taste in music."

"So are we serious, like a couple?" The words just appear, and as soon as they do, there's no taking them back. I wait.

"Zack, you're sweet, but you're a sophomore," Zaylee says after a few agonizing seconds. "I'll be in college next year. We're at different places in our lives."

This response is a major blow. "Can we at least talk in person?"

The silence that follows is excruciating.

"Come to the shop after my shift on Tuesday."

"Are you still mad about the mushrooms?"

"I'm not thrilled, but I'll get over it. Just remember, you're a genuine person, Zack."

"I will."

"See you Tuesday."

We hang up, but our short conversation keeps ricocheting in my mind like a deranged pinball game. I fully disappointed Zaylee by shrooming with Matthias. Still, two words she said give me hope: "genuine person." I have a chance to make things right, maybe even convince her I'm boyfriend material. But I have to act soon.

TWENTY-SIX

XO, ZACK

I'm on a mission: a solo bus journey to Yogurt Madness to win Zaylee's heart. It sounds cheesy, but this is what I've got to do. She needs to know I'm serious about her, about us.

I lean against the bus window and press play on my Discman. "MMMBop" by Hanson fills my ears. I'd never admit it to Matty (and it would probably get my Gilman membership card revoked), but this song gets me pumped up. I open my binder to the sheet of paper where I've been working on a love letter. Or at least a "let's get serious" note.

> *Dear Zaylee,*
> *I never thought I could connect with someone as quickly as I have with you. Since we met, I see things differently. You've helped me grow in so many ways. That's why I want to take the next step in our relationship. Even with the distance between us next year, let's give this a shot.*
> *Love,*
> *Zack*

I erase the last line and the closing since they both thoroughly suck. Love? That seems presumptuous. Maybe I should leave it simple and not try so hard to convince her. There's also the option of ditching the note entirely and improvising, but that's not my strong suit.

Think, Zack, not like a sophomore.

I pore over Dad's letter, searching for a few poetic pointers. The old man can string words together, and my Dylan Thomas knowledge did impress Zaylee. The bus deposits me, and the reality of the situation sets in. Screw a letter on binder paper—I need a decent card. And flowers.

There's a Safeway up the street, so I sprint over. The store lights are so bright they make me involuntarily blink upon entering. A quick scan and I find the greeting cards. As I thumb through the racks, I realize it's almost all corny crap, but I find one semi-acceptable option with a mountain sunset and the word "breathtaking" in fancy script on the front.

The message inside reads, "You're a view that takes my breath away." OK, that brings to mind a pair of silver-haired eighty-year-olds celebrating their gazillionth anniversary, but maybe a few personal touches can make it work. I grab a rose in a plastic container from the produce area, wet with condensation. Then I pay for everything and hightail it down the street.

My watch says I have a few minutes, so I sit on the curb and fill the inside of the card with my finest cursive.

Dear Zaylee,
I'm so glad you gave me a ride home that day. It was the best thing that's happened to me since moving to California. Let's turn this into something serious. I'm ready. Are you?
XO,
Zack

OK, now the whole thing feels inspired. I lick the seal on the envelope and taste sugary glue. Let's do this.

The minute Zaylee's shift ends, I'm leaning against the door to Yogurt Madness, rose and card behind my back. I watch as she hits the lights and locks up.

"Hey," I say.

"Let's get going." Zaylee is already walking over to the car and unlocking the doors with a beep.

We climb into the car, and she puts the key in the ignition. Before she starts the engine, I hand her the card and rose. "I got you these."

She looks down at the two items like they're alien artifacts. "What's this all about?"

"Just read the card."

She mouths "OK" and opens the envelope. It's not exactly the reaction I was hoping for.

I hold my breath as I watch Zaylee scan my clumsy attempt at eloquence. It probably only takes her a minute, but it feels like a century.

"Oh, Zack, you're sweet. I wasn't expecting anything like this." She closes the card and places it on her lap. "Look, you're a good guy."

Oh no. "What's the problem then?"

She looks out her window. "The problem is I'm gonna be eighteen in August. Our ages are going to be an issue when I'm away at school."

"You like me now, though, right?"

She looks down at the cheap drugstore rose. "Yes, you're fun and smart and cool. But you're a sophomore, Zack."

"Forget that. We can make this work." I'm playing a more confident, forceful version of myself, like one of the roommates on MTV's *The Real World.*

Zaylee opens the plastic container and sniffs the rose. "What would that even look like?"

"I'll visit you on weekends at school."

"What if I go out of state?

"Then we'll make plans for when you're home for the holidays."

But the time for rational explanation is over. This is my chance to show Zaylee that I can be a bold man of action. So, without any warning, I lean in and kiss her. She tastes like sprinkles.

For a few minutes, we lock lips and fumble around in the cold, dark Kia. Her hands go up my shirt—my fingers reach down tentatively and feel the lacy top of her underwear. With every kiss and stroke of her hair, I try to present the older, more assured version of me I'm imagining I can be. It's like I'm acting without words.

"OK," Zaylee whispers when we come up for air.

"OK, what?" I shift in the seat and adjust my pants. Things got pretty steamy here in the front seat.

"We'll see where this goes."

Hallelujah. My sappy card and heartfelt plea worked. "Does this mean you'll introduce me to your parents? Or at least tell them I exist."

"One step at a time, all-star."

"I'll take what I can get."

"And let me guess, at this moment, you need a ride?"

The solo bus ride was a solid independent move, but man, it's comfy in Zaylee's car. "I wouldn't say no."

She turns the engine on and starts in the direction of my home.

"There is so much happening in the world right now," she says while starting the car. "The Bill Clinton and Monica Lewinsky scandal, Russian citizens protesting Boris Yeltsin. If you're not outraged, you're not paying attention."

"Definitely." I'm half-listening and half-floating on a magic carpet of good vibes. I'm dying to tell someone about tonight—the card, the rose, all of it. I mean, I should be able to call Matty, but Zaylee is a sore subject between us.

I push the thought away because right now, in this car, as Zaylee lectures me about the Great Pacific Garbage Patch, I'm somewhere close to heaven. Of course, like any child of divorce, you're always waiting for the other shoe to drop. It's just a matter of when.

TWENTY-SEVEN
RAMPED UP

Matthias and I are taking one of what he calls "bonus lunches." We've been doing this periodically, skipping our fifth-period classes. It's no big thing for me since mine is Spanish II, and I have a solid 93%. Arizona prepped me well in the foreign language department.

There's a corner store with a deli a few blocks from the high school, so we pick up some sandwiches. Matthias is spitting out thoughts at one hundred miles a minute as we walk and eat.

"For real, my skating is ready to ascend to the next level. I've got plans, mega plans."

"Totally, man." I'm trying to sound sincere. But ever since we took mushrooms, I've wondered how much difference there is between Matthias when he's high and his actual personality. It's a conundrum.

He stops in his tracks. "Don't talk down to me, Zack. This is serious. I'm ready to get sponsored."

"I'm not arguing with you. Everyone knows you're the best skater at Berkeley High."

"Best skater in the Bay Area."

"OK, in the Bay Area."

"For real, I've been grinding in pools since I was a grommet after the '91 Oakland Hills Fire left all those houses vacant."

I look down. That was way before my time in California. I'm outclassed by his seniority.

"Watch this, Dr. Z." Matty throws his board on the ground and pushes off down the sidewalk. He does a smooth turn, flips his skate, and lands on it effortlessly. Then he rolls back over to where I'm standing.

"Once I get sponsored, I'll be in *Thrasher*, meet some legends like John Cardiel and Mike Carrol, do all that shit."

"Yeah, that would be awesome." I take a bite of my sandwich and keep walking. Matthias follows slowly on his skateboard.

"Not everything's easy for me like it is for you, Zack." He rolls up beside me. "My parents don't have a metric shit ton of money. You've been to my house."

"Dude, we don't even have a house."

"But look at your neighborhood compared to mine. I mean, your mom's a freakin' college professor."

Well, he has me there. Matty's neighborhood is grungier than ours, and we both know it. "You're kinda being a dick, Matthias."

"We're just talking, man. Chill. I'm giving it to you straight, letting you know how the social divide goes here in Berkeley."

This is the flip side of how honest we were on shrooms, when it was all about friendship, love, and connection.

"Dude, I can't even follow your logic when you're ramped up like this."

"Logic? Whatever, Zack. Since you started hanging with that girl, you've been so high on yourself."

"High on myself? Who's the one swaggering around

with his pants halfway off his ass, going, 'I should be sponsored'? You don't hear me talking about water polo scholarships or whatever."

In the space that follows, I hear a baby wailing a few blocks away. Matthias can be downright nasty when he's cornered, so I brace for whatever comes next. But instead, he shuts down.

We walk another block. After what feels like a Super Bowl-length commercial break, Matthias stops, pushes his bangs back, and gives me his most sincere, pleading look.

"You're right, Dr. Z. Sometimes I do act like a conceited idiot. I'm sorry." He swallows with a pronounced gulp. "Goddamn, they make a solid veggie sandwich."

"This turkey's good too."

Matthias kicks up his board and catches it by the top wheels. "You have to understand," he says, "that everyone knows you're one of the best polo players at school. Water polo is what gets popularity, betties, all of it."

I place a hand on his shoulder. "When I first saw you at the skatepark, I couldn't believe the tricks you were pulling off. You were skating like you were already sponsored." Even if I have no barometer for skating talent, my words come from the heart.

His eyes look watery. "Thanks, brother. I used to go to Embarcadero Plaza in the City and just watch the older skaters, dreaming of being one of them. Now I finally feel like I have a shot."

We hug spontaneously, but I break away before it feels too serious. I'm happy the worst is over; this wasn't exactly a fight, but it was the closest we've gotten to one.

"You want to see a water polo bro skate?"

I grab his board, drop it on the ground, and stand on it with my arms out like I'm about to surf a point break. After lurching around like a Weeble Wobble, I put my foot on the ground and attempt to propel myself forward. The board slips out from under me and starts rolling down the sidewalk out of control. I hit the ground, landing hard on my ass. I don't mind. It's funny.

"Dr. Z goes down!" Matthias cackles as I get up, and we both chase after his getaway skateboard.

For some reason, the sky decides to clear up at this moment. Rays of amber light hit Matthias's skin, giving him a trophy-colored glow. Once he catches up with his board, he wastes no time giving me a show. A few tic-tacs to pick up speed, a surprise switch in direction, then a glorious ollie that ends in a sidewalk smack that makes me flinch.

After a few minutes of his impromptu performance, I realize the sun is making me squint, leaving me with a dumb, fixed smile.

I'm glad we got past that conflict. Still, as I watch Matty skating, lost in his fantasies, a single question keeps pestering me. Sure, he's a good skater, but is he *that* good?

TWENTY-EIGHT
SHAPESHIFTING

It's almost midnight, and I should be asleep. Instead, I'm sitting up in bed listening to my mother talk about me.

"Our kid's thriving here—water polo, a girlfriend, the whole shebang."

Mom's trying to be quiet, but through the thin walls of the apartment, I can make out every word perfectly. Our floor plan doesn't provide much room for private conversation.

"Yes, water polo. Can you believe it, Silas?"

The name hits me like a golf club to the head. So, this is one of their mysterious check-ins. I can only describe this feeling as watching your life playing on a cruddy old VHS tape with large sections missing.

"Yes, he has friends," she says. "One, in particular, I'm not thrilled about."

Zaylee, Coach Reardon, now Mom. No one wants to give Matthias a break. Then I remember our argument earlier. Maybe he hasn't been the greatest influence. I mean, I wasn't taking mushrooms back in Tempe, was I? But one trip doesn't mean I'm going to hell in a handbasket.

"It's the age." She pauses to laugh at something my dad says, probably a witty anecdote from another era. "Zack won't tell me much unless I push, but he did read your letter."

Perched perfectly still, I wait through another long silence as Mom walks out of earshot. Eventually, I hear dishes clink, followed by her exasperated voice saying, "Silas, can we please discuss this another time?" Then things go quiet again until finally I hear her say, "OK, goodnight."

I clench all my muscles from head to toe and release them, but it doesn't do a goddamn thing to help me relax. Finally, I put the pillow over my head and take a few deep breaths. Soon my eyes start to close, and sleep overtakes me.

―――――

BAM BAM BAM

The pounding on our front door makes me jump. I roll over; the alarm clock reads half past three in the morning.

BAM...BAM BAM BAM...BAM

"Wake up, Dr. Z. It's your blood brother." Matthias is yelling at an obscene volume.

I fly out of bed. In my half-asleep state, the only plan is to reach the door before Matty wakes Mom, Geoff next door, and the whole flipping neighborhood.

"What the hell are you doing here?" I hiss through the screen door.

"I have to talk to you," he says, his voice a piercing fake whisper.

"It's 3:30 in the morning, dude."

His T-shirt is plastered to his torso with sweat, and his hair is sticking out in every direction. "Is your mom around?" Matthias cups his hands around his mouth. "Mrs. Coleman, I'd like to speak with you about an opportunity."

"Jesus, man. You have to quiet down."

Matthias ignores me; he's completely unhinged. "Mrs. Coleman, all I need is a few minutes of your time," he shouts. "Just hear me out."

His eyes are darting everywhere, and he can't stop moving. So, this is the Matthias everyone's been warning me about. I see my friend in there, but he's in and out—an animal shapeshifting.

"Did you skate the whole way here? That's nuts." Wrong word.

"BART wasn't running so I took the bus most of the way then skated the rest," he says in an unbroken outpouring. "Aren't you even going to invite me in, Zack?"

"If you can bring your voice down, we can—"

"Zack, what's going on out there? Do you know what time it is?" Mom pulls her robe tight around her. Somehow, she slept through the pounding, but our voices woke her.

I look down at my bare feet. "Matty's here."

"I see that." She approaches the screen door. "This is not a reasonable hour to be showing up on our doorstep, Matthias. Do your parents know you're out?"

Matthias darts away, paces the courtyard, then rebounds back to us. "Look," he says, squashing his nose against the screen. "Let me in, and I'll explain how my plan can work for all of us."

"Let me call your parents or a cab," my mother says firmly.

"They don't mind that I'm out. Please, can't I come in and share a life-changing proposal with you?"

Mom widens her eyes and takes me aside, behind the door where Matthias can't see us. "Is this normal behavior for your friend?"

Well, he *was* acting bizarre during our extended lunch—comparing our neighborhoods and going on about our supposed wealth. "Matthias is eccentric," I say into my mom's ear, "but this is a whole other level."

"And his parents let him stay out all hours?"

"They're pretty lax."

She sighs and opens the door.

Matthias bounds into our living room, speeding past me and taking center stage near the coffee table. It's surreal seeing him in our home out of nowhere.

"Mrs. Coleman—wait, here's the deal. I've been skating for a long time, and I'm super-mega-serious about it. Some people even call me Berkeley's best skater." He twirls his board in his arms, nearly hitting a lamp.

I walk over to him and pat a couch cushion. "Why don't you come on over and sit down, buddy."

Matthias takes a seat while continuing to spit out a nonstop blitz of ideas, his hands cutting the air like helicopter blades.

"Look, Mrs. Coleman, you understand that sports are important. I mean, you have a bona fide star under your roof." Matthias flashes a smile at me. "What I'm proposing, right here, right now, is that you invest in my skating talent."

The dude has only met my mother once, and he's trying to sell her on putting money into his nonexistent skateboarding career. I'm mortified—for him, me, Mom, Matty's family.

To Mom's credit, she doesn't flip out. She just glides into the kitchen and rustles around for the Yellow Pages.

Matthias's mind is racing like an Indy 500 car, bouncing from thought to thought, everything centered around skating. "What about getting in *Thrasher* magazine? Well, I'm glad you asked. What we'll do is take out a full page and get people interested in seeing me skate."

An ad for what? For him? He's not making sense.

In the other room, I hear my mom talking in hushed tones to a cab service. "That's correct," she says. "We have a young man here who needs a ride home."

"You see, my family is hella supportive in words but can't help me financially. That's when I came up with my plan."

I think of Oscar driving us to the Gilman concert with the Clash playing on the VW stereo. Seems like another life. Wish I could get back to that feeling.

"Mrs. Coleman," Matthias shouts towards the kitchen. "Do you have money to invest in getting a young athlete's career off the ground? I promise you'll make it back and more when I'm sponsored."

I groan. "Dude, please stop with all that."

The front door is still open, and the cold air raises goose-bumps on my forearms. I look over to the kitchen and catch Mom's eye for a second as Matthias babbles in the background.

Mom approaches the couch as if she's walking up to a puma in the wild. Suddenly, our house feels like an emergency zone, a crime scene, the setting for something serious and dangerous.

"You're back," Matthias says with a giant grin. "So, Zack must have told you I love music. Another part of my plan is to have NOFX play at an event. I figured you would have some connections at Cal. Greek Theater might be too big, but who knows? Maybe we throw a festival like Warped Tour."

My mom sits next to our visitor and takes his hand in hers. "Matthias," she begins, "it's too late at night for us to have this conversation."

She pats his hand as Matty keeps talking about what he's going to charge for tickets and the percentage we'll keep. Mom just keeps nodding and repeating "OK" in a soothing voice. He eventually starts to peter out. The gaps between his words grow longer, and the laps around the mental race-track get slower.

"A taxi is on its way," my mom says. "You're going home now. Is that clear?"

"Uh-huh," Matthias replies like he's under a spell. "I guess we can talk about my skating another time."

"For sure, man," I interject.

"Mrs. Coleman, can we talk about my plan later?"

"Let's just get you home."

No wonder Mom is so good at calming Matthias down; she did this same thing for years with my dad. What's weird is I'm slightly jealous of the attention she's giving him.

"You're not mad, are you?"

"No one's mad," I tell Matthias, squeezing his puny bicep.

The phone rings. Mom places Matthias's hand down lightly and walks evenly to the kitchen. "He'll be right out," she tells the dispatch person. "Zack, why don't we walk Matthias to his ride?" Pure acting. She needs her own TV show.

"Want me to grab your board, Matty? You must be exhausted from skating here."

Matthias stands, his shoulders dropping like a rag doll. He hands his board to me without a fight. "It wasn't that bad," he says, stifling a yawn. "I bussed some of the way here."

I imagine taking public transit from Matty's neighbor-hood in the post-midnight hours. No thanks.

Mom continues her Emmy-level performance. "That's a long way to come, and at night too." She hands me two twenty-dollar bills, and our eyes meet for a second. He's your responsibility, she expresses without words.

We exit into the brisk night air, and I shepherd him along

until we reach the taxi waiting at our curb. "Matty, do you know your home address for the driver?"

Matthias gives me a bitter look. "I'm not drunk, dude. I know what's happening. You're kicking me out."

The driver rolls down the passenger window, sending out a bouquet of cigarette butts and air freshener. "Please get my friend here home," I tell the unshaven, bleary-eyed cabbie and hand him the money my mom gave me. "He's had a crappy night."

I settle Matthias into the back seat, where he looks out the window, dazed. "Take care, buddy."

No answer. From the curb, I watch the cab peel off. Then I walk slowly back inside, spent.

"Your friend is on his way home?" Mom's no longer performing or comforting anyone. She's in business mode, and it scares the living shit out of me.

"Yeah, the cab just left." I'm highly aware of the ambient refrigerator noise at this moment.

"Go get some sleep," Mom says. "We'll sift through this mayhem tomorrow."

I retreat to my bedroom with shame, fury, and bewilderment churning inside of me. Everything is broken; nothing makes sense. I know that after tonight, Matthias and I will never be the same again.

TWENTY-NINE
GRAND PRIZE IN FAILURE

What do you do after the person you considered your best friend showed up at your front door in a delirious state, begging your single, working parent to support his destiny as a pro skateboarder?

If you're my mother, you avoid talking about it, which is way scarier than her blowing up.

"Come straight home after school," she says and screws the cap tightly on her coffee thermos. "That is *not* a request."

Then she's out the door before I can even come up with a snappy retort.

Usually, my morning walk to school empties the nasty gunk out of my head, but not today. On no sleep and with the 3:00 a.m. disaster on loop, it's like marching through mud. I've been trying so hard to keep Matthias's mess out of our life, yet somehow, it's exploding over everything. What happens now? Who is Zack Coleman at Berkeley High if he's not Matthias Alexander's friend?

I slump into my seat for English and pull my beat-up library copy of *The Catcher in the Rye* by J.D. Salinger from my backpack. I love this book; it's so absorbing I can't help but read beyond the assigned chapters.

"Why is Holden so angry at the world?" Mrs. Garcia asks us.

The whole room explodes into boisterous shouting; our teacher encourages lively discussion.

"Because he's lazy and spoiled," someone yells.

"He must have had horrendous parenting."

"Who cares? *Catcher in the Rye* is full of outdated teenage stereotypes."

"Holden's jealous," I hear myself say, and for some reason, everyone shuts up. "He wants what everybody else has but can't admit it to himself."

Mrs. Garcia points at me. "Bingo."

Class ends, and I amble aimlessly into lunch. I didn't realize how locked into the groove of hanging around Matthias and company I'd become. After last night, the bleachers feel like they're blocked off with yellow tape for me, but I head over anyway, hoping to see Matty and sort things out.

I find Rob and Tina showing each other basic skating tricks, but there's no sign of Matthias. Everything is the same, except it isn't.

Tina screeches to a stop on her board. "Yo, Desert Rat."

"No one calls me that anymore."

"Bro, I'm only kidding. Does being a water polo hero make you uptight?" She takes a swig from a Dr. Pepper can.

"Check this out!" Rob jumps off a broken piece of cinder block. He looks like he's dropped some pounds while I wasn't paying attention. The PowerBar diet must be working.

"Nice one," Tina yells.

Her eyes flicker with admiration. She's a far better skater than Rob, but that's not the point. There's a spark between them. Tina and Rob are a couple now. Everyone's falling in love. What is this, *Beverly Hills 90210*?

"You guys seen Matthias?"

"He wasn't in health," Tina says while skating in a circle around us.

Rob kicks his board into his hands, a sloppy imitation of Matthias's signature move. "I figured you'd know. You guys are best buddies or whatever."

"No. Haven't seen him today." There's no way I'm telling these two what happened at my house last night. And I don't care if Rob is still pissed at me for waltzing in and claiming his old friend. Now we've both lost Matthias.

The three of us stare at each other in strained silence.

I've got no desire to hang with Rob and Tina without Matthias. And they sure as hell don't seem to want my friend-stealing ass around. The two of them see right through me for the phony I am.

"Catch you later," I say.

So here I am, eating soggy spaghetti in the cafeteria by myself, just like I feared I would way back on my first day. The difference is now I don't mind being alone all that much. It would almost be tranquil if there weren't two questions on repeat in my mind: Where the hell is Matthias? And what will my mom do to me when I get home?

———

So, I wish I could say I disobeyed my mom, stopped by Matty's house after school to check on him, and patched things up with my best friend. But alas, I'm a coward. Instead, I walk home exactly as instructed to find she's not even here.

Racing thoughts. Churning stomach.

Even the familiar sticky black cushion of my weight

bench is no comfort. I grip the cold, ridged bar and lift it off the stand, hoping for a hint of salvation. One rep, two reps. I keep going, waiting for the thoughts to stop. No luck.

Clank. I sit up and wipe my brow.

I call Zaylee. Talking to her always makes me feel human again.

"There's a conference happening in Japan next month. It's all about reducing the emission of gases that contribute to global warming," she informs me with unbridled excitement.

"I like hearing you angry about the environment. Makes me wish I was more involved."

"You *should* be angry," Zaylee says. "Our world is heating up, and we have to do something. Not even for us— for our kids."

"We're going to have kids?"

She laughs. "I mean, our generation's kids."

I try to listen, but I'm too distracted by my personal drama. "I have something weird to tell you."

"Weird? You? I can't believe it."

"Very funny. It's about Matthias, so don't get pissed."

"Let me guess, more magic mushrooms?"

"No, that was the last of that." I take a deep breath. "Matty showed up at my house at three in the morning and asked my mom to give him money."

"Money? For what?"

"To become a pro skateboarder."

Zaylee bursts into laughter. Like, she's seriously cracking up.

"It's not funny. I think Matthias had a psychotic break or something."

"That guy is so sketchy. He loitered at Yogurt Madness for months, trying to get my number."

"Didn't I do the same thing—wait around to get your number?"

"In your case, it was endearing. You were cute."

The last word pulls me out of my funk. "You thought I was cute?"

"We've been over this," Zaylee says. "Cute and caring. Good combo."

"Well, you're a caring girlfriend."

"Zack, we haven't used that word yet."

"But we talked about us in your car." I try to quell the quiver in my voice. "You read my card and everything."

For the next thirty seconds, I swear I can hear Zaylee thinking, and it's terrifying. Finally, she says, "You need to meet my parents. We'll do it over winter break."

"That would be awesome," I sputter. Being invited into her genuine life—not sneaking around on pseudo-dates. This is the moment I've been dreaming of.

"Zack, I don't mean to be bitchy about Matthias."

"I know—"

She cuts me off. "But it's not OK that anyone holds so much power over you."

"It's true. It's like I've been under a spell or something." I remember Matthias talking about Crowley and shudder a little. I did some internet research on that guy, and it turns out he was like some freaky magician Led Zeppelin was obsessed with.

"Matthias is lucky to have you as a friend, not the other way around. Don't ever forget it."

"I won't forget."

"Promise?"

"I promise."

After hanging up, I waste time every way I can without leaving the house: watching reruns of *The Simpsons*, doing leg reps, stress-eating Ben and Jerry's Cherry Garcia. After an eternity, my mom walks through the front door, dog-eared textbooks and student papers spilling from her over-stuffed bag.

"Not an easy day of classes on a decent night of sleep." She sighs, depositing her things on the counter. "And last night's sleep was *far* from decent." She sits beside me and lifts the empty ice cream container off the coffee table. "Sugar relief?"

I shrug. "Look, Mom, Matthias has never done anything like that before."

Mom places her hand on my knee—never a good sign. "You don't need to apologize for his behavior last night. That was entirely out of your control."

Here comes the "but."

"He's a troubled young man. I understand he's your friend—"

"Matthias has a good side." I'm feeling tears coming—lack of sleep is catching up with me. "You should see him with his kid brother, Noel. He's been there for me too."

She looks toward the front door, and I can almost see her replaying last night. "I appreciate that he took you under his wing when you were new."

"Matty is the most open-minded person I've ever met."

She pats my hand. "I don't doubt that for a second, kiddo. We make choices when we're in new environments that we might not otherwise."

I wipe my eyes on my shirt. "You sound like Coach Reardon."

"Look, us adults don't know how to deal with the uncomfortable stuff any better than kids. We flounder and try our best." Mom pulls my head onto her shoulder. She smells like a mixture of patchouli and perfume.

"The way your friend acted last night, did that remind you of anyone?"

I knew the answer before she finished asking the question. "Yes. Dad."

"The mania, how he petered out—I've been on that ride far too many times." She stands, takes the Ben and Jerry's, and walks into the kitchen, where she tosses the container into the garbage can below the sink. "It makes sense you'd be attracted to someone like that, with your father out of the picture."

"Mom, that sounds like Psychology 101."

In the living room light, I can see the bags under her eyes. "Zack, there's a good chance your friend Matthias is bipolar. But you knew that, didn't you?"

Bipolar. It's a term I've heard thrown around like an insult on TV shows and in movies, but it never seemed a part of my reality. I don't even know what it means exactly.

"Guess so," I admit, putting pieces I'd ignored together —Declan, Coach Reardon, my instincts. "So, is Dad bipolar too? Is that why he would just disappear for days?"

"I think Silas likely has the same diagnosis. Unfortunately, he was unwilling to talk with a psychiatrist or counselor about anything he was experiencing or how it affected our family."

"Selfish."

She sighs. "His mood would go up and up and up until he crashed savagely. Then he just drifted into his lectures, poems, and books like nothing happened."

"I remember. Even when he'd leave the house for days, Dad never explained shit when he came home. Just went to his study."

"He kept me up plenty of nights wondering if he even *would* come back. It was easy to pretend it was a midlife crisis." She looks down at her hands which are gripped together so tightly they're turning white.

"He was stubborn," she continues. "The real reason we

divorced was Silas's unwillingness to work on himself. But he's a good person, your father. And your friend Matthias could be a good person as well. I just don't know."

"He is a good person." My voice comes out like a horse's whinny.

"Play whatever sport you like, date who you want, but you have to tell Matthias you're not going to be able to hang out anymore. At least not until he's getting psychiatric support."

Mom made the call; it's out of my hands now. "This is bullshit. Yes, Matty messed up, but he isn't a monster. He has problems, like everyone, like me."

"I know this feels unfair, but sometimes parents know things, even when they don't want to."

Now it's my turn to strike a blow. "Speaking of Dad, when do we discuss what you two talk about in your secret conversations?"

She walks towards her bedroom. "I'm exhausted. We'll deal with that another time."

Perfect. More procrastination. "I'm going to hold you to that."

"I know you will," she says from the other side of the wall, her voice small and creaky.

I click the remote, and the *Friends* theme song kicks in. The irony is killing me. Friends are supposed to be there for each other. We went from best buddies to enforced separation in a few months. That must be some kind of world record, like taking home the grand prize in failure.

THIRTY
RIGHTEOUS ANGER

Someone should write a book entitled *How to Break Up with Your Best Friend*. For the last few days, I've been wandering the halls of Berkeley High in a daze, stewing on the traitorous deed my mother assigned me. I'm a mess, thoughts colliding into each other like over-filled freight trains.

Loyalty dictates that you deliver a blow like this face-to-face, but Matthias stopped showing up at school. He vanished like a skinny ghost vapor, slipping back into the dimension he came from.

I even decide to check my stupid Hotmail account in the computer lab to see if he wrote me an email. Nope.

Feeling nostalgic for better days, I finally look up Angela Davis from the poster at Matty's house. According to Ask Jeeves, she lived all over the world, taught controversial secret classes to college students, and even went to prison. Angela Davis' fearlessness makes me feel even more like a piece of shit for abandoning Matthias in his hour of need.

After school, Zaylee scoops me up, and we head to the library to study. "Was your Mom furious about your late-night visitor?"

"I don't even want to talk about it. The whole thing is so embarrassing."

She slaps my arm. "You can tell me anything, dummy—you know that. Even your friendship soap opera stuff."

We pass a school bus packed with rambunctious youngsters. Man, life was easier back when I was a kid. "My mom told me I can't hang out with Matty anymore," I say. "She says he's got too much heavy stuff going on, which is total horseshit."

"She's looking out for you, Zack."

"That doesn't mean she gets to dictate who my friends are."

"Sounds like he's in a crisis or just can't regulate his behavior."

"It's not Matty's fault that he gets riled up like that," I say. "I think he's bipolar."

The word hangs in the stuffy car like a spoiled bag of takeout food. Zaylee pulls into the parking lot and finds a spot in front of the library.

"You're right," she says, her voice gentler now. "No one should blame Matthias for being bi, tripolar, or whatever he is. That's not his fault. It's just brain chemistry."

Zaylee strokes my cheek and leaves her hand there. It's cool and smells of jasmine hand lotion.

I shut my eyes. "It's not just the bipolar thing, though. Matty messes with my head in other ways. Around him, I end up doing stuff I didn't plan on doing."

"I've seen it happening," she says. "Friendship doesn't have to be easy, but it shouldn't make you miserable, either."

We sit in the car like that for a few minutes, just breathing, her warm palm on my face. Then we walk hand in hand into the library. Inside, Zaylee walks over to a Recommended Reading display and points at a book called *Race Matters* by Cornel West.

"This is essential reading. Dr. West is a genius." Zaylee sits at a study table. "I'm going to jot a few things down for this presentation I'm giving to the lower grades."

"Dang, can't think of the last time I did extra work for school."

"You have your passions. I have mine."

I leave my brilliant girlfriend to her studies and slink over to the information desk. "Do you have any books about being bipolar?" I ask a man in a brown turtleneck behind a computer. "Like, psychological issues. Stuff like that."

"We have some titles on bipolar disorder," he answers in the perfect librarian voice. "Psychology is over there." The man points to a row halfway across the room.

I thank him and walk over so fast I almost knock over two girls in Backstreet Boys shirts on the way. The Psychology section is gigantic. Turns out there are books on every conceivable topic relating to the human mind.

I scan the shelf in a panic until one title jumps out at me: *Mood Disorders: How to Understand What You or Your Loved One is Experiencing*. Flipping to the index, I see it lists at least a dozen pages with the word bipolar.

I sit on the floor with the book open. My chest feels hollow as I take in the words.

Accelerated speech. Restlessness. Overconfidence. This is Matthias to a T.

I keep reading. So, bipolar disorder used to be called manic depression (which I've heard a million times on TV), but that term is outdated. Scientists and doctors don't know what causes it, but probably a blend of "genetics, environment, and brain chemistry." According to the book, medication and therapy are the best treatments. Psychedelic mushrooms are not listed.

"What are you reading?"

Zaylee's voice takes me by surprise, and I rise too quickly from the floor. Bad idea—my legs are asleep.

"I looked in the Sports section, but you were nowhere to be found."

"You do realize I have other interests?"

"I'm only joshing you," she says and kisses my nose. "You make it too easy. Mood disorders, huh?"

Zaylee tries to take the book, but I slip it back where I found it on the shelf. "Just trying to understand Matty better, I guess."

"Because you're a good human."

"Will you give this good human a ride home?"

She crosses her arms. "When are you getting your license again?"

I put my arm around her shoulders and steer us across the library floor. "Cut me some slack, OK? This is a transitional time."

"You sound like a guidance counselor."

"Ha. I'm the last person anyone should come to for advice."

"Don't sell yourself short, Mr. Coleman."

We exit the library and enter the soft afternoon light. As we approach the car, I catch sight of our distorted reflection in the windshield, and Zaylee and I look like a perfect couple. This is what the romantic in me has been dreaming of for years. I wish I wasn't so preoccupied by the other situation I have going on.

I may be changing, learning, and maturing, but I've still got a shitty-ass deed to do. And I've got to do it soon.

———

I've been doing pushups, splashing cold water on my face, eating stale Cheetos—every procrastination activity I can think of—but you can't delay the inevitable. Eventually, I end up in my bedroom staring at the phone. Mom's not home, so I have the space to do this and not feel under her microscope. The moment has arrived. I pick up the 3000-pound receiver and start pushing the buttons of Matthias's number. One by one by one.

"Zack." Oscar's soft inflection tells me he knows why I'm calling. "Haven't seen you for a while, buddy. Since I drove you youngsters to that punk show."

"Things have been hectic. You know how polo season is." Here I go, lying right from the start.

Brief silence. "Well, I know Matthias will be anxious to hear from you. Let me get him."

My heart thumps through my Yellowjackets sweatshirt. I pull at the strings, and the hood draws snugly around my face, muffling all sounds like a warm cocoon.

"Sup, Dr. Z." Matthias sounds tired and groggy, nothing like the whirling dervish in my living room a few nights ago.

"Hey, Matty. Haven't seen you at school."

He exhales slowly. "Well, I had one of my episodes."

No kidding. "Were your parents pissed about you being out so late at our house?"

"No, they don't trip too hard about that," he replies. "It's more that they want me under proper medical supervision. My doctor upped my meds like she always does and told me to take as long as I need to get my head together. So, that's what I'm doing."

We both go silent. The words "medical supervision" weigh the conversation down like iron chains.

"You caught me off guard the other night, showing up

like that. But to be real, I'd been wondering if something was up. The last few weeks, you were acting different."

"Look, man. When I'm on the upswing, it feels amazing. I just want to talk and talk. I'm sorry if I was out of hand."

I remember seeing something about euphoria in that mood disorders book. "You don't need to be sorry," I tell him. "I think I understand."

He scoffs. "Yeah, I bet."

"Matty, I told you all about my dad. And I've been reading up on bipolar disorder."

"This shit isn't a book, dude. It's my life, and I've been dealing with it for years."

His words are slurry and running into each other, nothing like the smooth, in-control guy I remember from the beginning of the school year.

"So what happens now?"

"I'm gonna chill for a minute. Go back to the counselor I used to see back in middle school."

He's being so forthcoming, which makes me feel even more horrible. "Matty, look, this is impossible." The phone is slippery in my hand. "I want us to go back to normal, but my mom is coming down hard on me."

"Zack, I said I was sorry."

"I'm supposed to cut things off with you. We can't hang out anymore."

It gets quiet again, and I can hear A Tribe Called Quest playing in my head, which makes me choke up.

"Can't say I'm surprised," Matthias says eventually.

"I know it's bullshit."

"You're not a baby, Desert Rat. Your mom is way too controlling. Grow some balls." He lets that one sink in.

"My mom's been through the wringer and doesn't need any more stress."

"But I do? You're so fucking spoiled, dude. I just needed a leg up, and you treated me like trash."

Here we go again with the woe-is-me stuff. I have to turn this around. "Matthias, you're an amazing person."

"Fuck that noise," he hisses. "You thought I was cool before you knew anyone here and had no status. Now that you've got a girl and the polo team, you're kicking me to the curb."

"This has nothing to do with any of that."

"Like hell it doesn't. I showed you Telegraph and taught you about punk rock." He sounds like a wounded animal. "Guided you on our mushroom trip. This is how you thank me?"

"You know I appreciate that, Matty."

"Don't call me that. Nicknames are for blood brothers." The rage is rising in his voice, slicing through the lethargic drawl. "You're a fucking poseur."

The word is a kick in the stomach. The line goes so quiet that the only sounds I hear are the beeping of a video game and Noel laughing in the background.

"We can't be friends right now," I say after calming myself down. "It's not entirely my choice. But I know it's the right thing."

He's not even listening anymore. "Friends don't abandon each other. And don't think for a second I don't see Zaylee's part in this." Under his breath, I hear the word "bitch."

That's it. "Matthias, we're done."

"Don't worry. We were done the minute you met her." And with that, he hangs up on me. All that anger and bitterness—his, mine, ours—have left me exploding with adrenaline, like I just wrestled or had a two-hour polo scrimmage. I curl my fingers into fists until my fingernails cut into my palms.

"You idiot!"

I yell it at Matthias, Mom, Dad, Coach Reardon, and especially myself—so loud I bet the whole complex can hear. Screw everyone.

Exhausted, I fall back on my pillow and gaze at the smooth gray paint on the ceiling.

I pull *The Catcher in the Rye* from the bedside table and lose myself in Holden's righteous anger until I pass out with the book on my chest.

THIRTY-ONE
CAREFREE HIGH SCHOOL SPECIMENS

I slept like hell and start my walk to school in a fog of regret and sadness. Even some welcome morning sunshine can't bolster my mood. Today's the day I stop looking for Matthias on campus. He's going to be AWOL for the foreseeable future, and what would I even say after our last horrific conversation?

That's right. Since our friend breakup last night, I'm back where I started: alone at Berkeley High. I'd been living in the Matty punk skater bubble. I've got Zaylee, but no one here even knows she exists. Nope, I've got to fend for myself again, and it sucks.

The day feels like a thousand years. Kids are laughing, flirting, fighting—acting like teens. I feel like I'm watching through filthy Plexiglas.

"What's up, home skillet?"

"Talk to the hand."

"As if. I wouldn't go out with him if he owned a yacht and looked like Freddie Prinze Jr."

I can't relate to these carefree high school specimens today. My world is a colorless, friendless vacuum.

At some point between lunch and sixth period, I realize there's only one answer. It's time to surrender to the inevitable and become the full-fledged jock that Coach Reardon wants me to be.

So, even though he gets under my skin, I need to make peace with Declan Duffy. We both get intensely competitive during practice, but I have to admit, the guy never seems to hold a grudge. In fact, I've been turning down his invites since the beginning of the year.

I approach him in the locker room after practice. "Good work in the pool, man."

Declan looks up from tying his shoe. "You too."

"What are you guys up to right now?" I shove a hand in the front pocket of my jeans and rest the other against the cold steel of the lockers.

Declan scratches his armpit. "Not much. Some of us go to McDonald's and shoot the shit after practice."

"Mind if I tag along?" *Damn, that sounded desperate.*

He tosses his backpack over his shoulder. "Don't you need to see what your skateboarder boyfriend has to say?"

My neck muscles tense, and I feel a powerful urge to clothesline him right here and now.

Declan's henchman, a bulky guy with a bowl cut named Tony Torres, appears in a towel. His pecs are way more prominent than mine.

"My buddy has some classes with Matthias Alexander," Tony says. "That dude stopped showing up at school."

My ears perk up, ravenous for details.

"Yeah, I heard that too," Declan adds.

Tony pulls his hoodie over his head and shakes his arms into the sleeves. "Freaked out on drugs or something."

Declan laughs like Tony made the best joke he's ever heard.

"Bro, we've known Matthias since grade school," Declan

says. "He started taking LSD in kindergarten. That's why I had to warn you. Yellowjackets look out for each other."

I follow them out of the locker room, feeling like the world's biggest fraud. "Thanks for the heads up. Guess I got sucked into skater world for a while there."

"No biggie. You wouldn't know about him. I mean, you're still new here."

For some reason, that makes me bristle. "I pick things up fast. Never even played water polo before this year."

"For sure," Declan says. "Everyone knows you're a monster in the pool."

We end up at McDonald's, where the guys slip into a greasy booth in the back to devour Big Macs and run through the same topics on repeat: upcoming games, raging keggers, and what girls at Berkeley High have the best bodies.

"How about you?" Tony asks, between slurps of milk-shake. "You must be drowning in ass—new polo player from out of town and all."

I remember Zaylee telling me about a book called *The Feminine Mystique*. It's safe to say these guys aren't schooled in women's liberation. "I'm dating someone."

"Yo, Coleman has a lady," Tony says. "Who?"

"She's a senior at Bishop O'Dowd," I answer and bite down on my burger.

Tony laughs so hard I can see right into his mushy french-fry-filled mouth. "What a heap of crap," he says.

"She's coming to the Mill Valley game," I say and take a long, slow sip of Diet Coke.

Declan tosses a fry into his mouth. "We'll see."

After a few more grueling minutes with Captain Crude and his cronies, I tell them I have to duck out to go home and study.

"See you at the game, Coleman," Tony says.

Declan gives me two thumbs up and a sarcastic smile. "Tell your senior girlfriend we can't wait to meet her."

"Later."

Neanderthals. If this is the thrilling part of high school athletics I've been missing out on, well, Coach Reardon, I gave it a shot. Declan may not be my sworn enemy, but he's far from a friend.

By the time I get home, I'm so lonely and homesick that I decide to call Miguel. It's been months since I've checked in with the guy. I've been so wrapped up in Mattyworld that everything else faded away. Figure I should let him know I'm still alive.

"So what's the 411, man?"

"Dude," he says, barely able to contain himself. "I've got a girlfriend, Louisa. You have to meet her when you visit Tempe."

Don't see that happening any time soon. "I've been dating someone too. Her name is Zaylee."

"Check us out, man. Both of us with girlfriends."

"Crazy, right?"

"So, no wrestling?" Miguel asks.

"Nah, I play water polo, though."

"You hang out with your teammates, or do you have other friends?"

"This one dude, Danny Chang, is pretty cool. He's a stoner, but he introduced me to some skaters I used to kick it with."

"Woah, skaters," he says, sounding sort of scared. "That's a different crowd for you."

"Well, California is nothing like Tempe."

I bet I sound like a prick to him, but I don't even care. I'm not ready to say anything about Matthias or what's been going on in my life. Talking to Miguel is like flipping through an old yearbook. It's hard to be cool with someone who knew me before I had armpit hair.

THIRTY-TWO
THAT'S ADOLESCENCE

ER is nothing to get too worked up about, just a TV hospital drama, but Mom loves this show, especially George Clooney. And even though I'm still irate about her forbidding me to see Matthias, I creep out of my bedroom after finishing my homework to join her on the couch.

"What do you think about me coming to see you play polo this weekend?" she asks as a Juicy Fruit ad starts.

"You mean in Mill Valley? We're playing Tamalpais High School."

"C'mon, it'll be like the old days." She socks me lightly on the shoulder. "I used to watch you wrestle all the time."

"It's a hike to Marin County," I say. "And they're not our supreme rivals, like Acalanes High School or Gunn in Palo Alto, but it'll still be a good game." It's fun showing off my local knowledge.

"Perfect. Well, I need a road trip. Maybe Geoff will want to come."

The phone rings, interrupting our first semi-pleasant exchange in a while. "Will you answer that? I simply cannot stir from this couch."

I get up and grab the phone. It's not like I'm following *ER* anyway; too much is happening in my head.

"How are you doing, big guy?" It's Oscar Alexander on the other end.

So, here we are. What do you tell the parent of the kid your mother demanded you cut off? Your blood brother. Your ex-best friend. You take a breath and say, "Pretty good. Watching TV."

"Great, Zack. Tell you what," Oscar says, sounding uneasy, "will you get your mother on the phone?"

"Sure, Mr. Alexander. One sec." I cover the mouthpiece. "It's Matthias's dad," I whisper. "I have no idea what he wants."

Mom walks over and takes the phone from me. "Hello?"

Here's what I hear:

"Yes, I understand…that tends to happen at this age…I know Matthias is struggling…Zack is going through a lot as well…"

It goes on and on like this. I wave both hands to get Mom's attention and mouth, "What the hell is this about?"

She shushes me.

This is too weird. I escape to my room but can still make out Mom's side of the conversation.

"That's right…for now…it's the best choice for our family…Zack needs to focus on school and his athletics… Mr. Alexander—Oscar, your son showed up on our doorstep at 3:30 in the morning to solicit money from me…this is the first time you and I have ever spoken…well, I appreciate that…let's let things settle down for a while…"

Finally, I hear the plastic clank of her replacing the phone on the receiver and return to the living room. "I can't believe that just happened," I tell her. "It's the worst when parents call other parents to talk."

"That was a deeply distressing conversation."

"Mom, tell me what he said." Sitting helpless while she and Oscar talked was about as comfortable as dancing in my underwear in front of homeroom.

"From what Oscar—Mr. Alexander—related, well, it's clear your friend misses you a great deal."

"Matty hasn't shown up at school. Did Oscar mention that little detail?"

Mom removes her glasses, letting them dangle around her neck on their string. "Oscar said," she begins, "that Matthias is recuperating after a manic episode, so they're giving him space. His teachers are sending packets home."

Why does she suddenly sound sympathetic? "They upped his medication, too," I mutter.

"Oscar mentioned something to that effect."

"So what did he want from you?"

Mom looks me in the eye. "Oscar wants me to reconsider and let you spend time with Matthias. He feels Matthias needs you, and you're a good influence on him."

I snort.

"Do you believe you are? A good influence?"

"As much as anyone can be on Matthias."

"Well," she continues, "Oscar told me you tutored him in chemistry. Is that true?"

God, the afternoon Matthias and I studied at Slice of Life feels like a hundred years ago. "He was struggling in chem, so we ran questions about ionic and covalent bonds."

Her eyes cloud up around the edges. "Regardless of my bias for science, that was a lovely thing to do."

"So, what did you finally decide? With Oscar."

"As much as I sympathize with what their family is dealing with, that child is a quagmire of problems. So I told him no."

A commercial for AOL comes on the TV showing shiny, happy people on computers while a voice tries to persuade me to call 1-800-4-Online. America Online is relentless with its advertising.

"But I understand he means a lot to you," she says. "Just let this breathe for a minute. Trust me."

I clear my throat. "Mom, I resent adults telling me what friendships I can have. It's bullshit, and it keeps happening. Coach Reardon, now you."

She shrugs. "That's adolescence, kiddo. At eighteen, you can do whatever you want."

I want to holler at the top of my lungs, rip into her about how we keep tiptoeing around our own issues. But it's almost 10:30, and I'm too worn out for any more drama. I start toward my room, but not without a parting shot.

"This is about more than Matthias, and you know it. It's about you keeping things from me. About Dad."

I pull my door closed. Not exactly a slam, but hard enough to make a point.

"I'm looking forward to watching you play tomorrow," Mom's muffled voice says, glossing over my accusation.

I don't reply. But the truth is, despite all the mess and secrets and anger, I want her there too.

THIRTY-THREE
THE UTTER FLAWLESSNESS OF THE MOMENT

At 6:30 a.m., I wake up to a glittering Berkeley sunrise. First, stretches and weights. Then, I take a cold shower to keep my energy up for the pool. I'm always nervous before games or matches, and today is a bigger deal than usual. It's an away game, and I've got family coming, not to mention Zaylee.

I pack my bag with my Speedo, water polo cap, *The Catcher in the Rye*, Discman, and two CDs: Bad Religion and Goo Goo Dolls. One to get me pumped, one to help me think about life.

On my way out the door, I find Mom absorbed in the crossword puzzle with the paper spread across the dining room table.

"I'm off to campus to meet up with the team. Are you still planning to make it today?"

"Hmm?" She looks up from the paper, her nightgown revealing a chest freckled by years in the Arizona sun. I look away; you don't stare at your mother's body for too long. That's just weird.

"I asked if you're coming to Mill Valley. Like you said last night."

"Absolutely. What time does the game start again?" She shakes the paper, then folds it over, leaning closer to the puzzle.

I tap the flyer on the fridge. "We play at noon. I left the info here, like the old days."

"Sounds good, kiddo." She wrinkles her forehead. "Zack, can you think of a six-letter word for an animal in John Wayne movies? This one is eluding me."

I stop and picture The Duke in full cowboy attire, all macho and in command, staring out over the miles of barren terrain. Out of the blue, the answer pops into my mind. "Try bovine."

My mom scratches the letters in with her pen. "That works perfectly," she says. "You're a genius."

"What can I say? I'm a Renaissance man." With that, I push open the screen door and start my jog to Berkeley High, playing out potential polo scenarios to focus my mind.

A few fellas are loading onto the school bus when I arrive, and I can see some others through the windows. Coach Reardon slaps me on the back. "Rise and shine, Coleman," he says. "You ready to do this?"

Did the old man just smile at me? "You know it, Coach." I hop inside and claim a seat behind the driver to avoid nausea.

"Hey, Coleman," Declan yells from the back, where he's holding court with Tony and some other dudes. "You freaked out to start in front of your senior girlfriend?"

My ears burn like Arizona asphalt. Why did I even tell them Zaylee was coming? There was no point in seeing these numbnuts outside of practice. Fine, they're the popular kids, but their maturity level is *Captain Underpants*-level at best.

"Not too worried about it, dude," I reply with all the cool I can muster. "Just concentrating on playing a good game."

"A good game," Tony yells. "And an extra-good post-game." Both boys crack up, and I hear the loud slap of palms giving high fives.

I crack open *Catcher* and read a few pages while the bus pulls out of the lot. Soon, the early morning catches up with me, and I'm snoozing with my head against the window, drooling on my sweatshirt.

I wake up forty-five minutes later just as we're crossing the Golden Gate Bridge. Mom and I went into SF— "the City," as everyone calls it—on a few tourist trips, but today is my first time going to Marin County. Alcatraz, the fog, the hulking burnt-orange cables just outside the window—I'm overwhelmed by the abundant beauty in every direction. For the first time in days, something is taking my mind off my Matthias guilt.

I feel the thud-thud-thud of the wind from an open window a few seats back. As the bus speeds along the free-way, I picture Zaylee in the stands watching me play, her eyes shining with pride. Life seems boundless. I pop on the Goo Goo Dolls CD and skip to "Name." It fits my mood to a T.

When we arrive, Coach Reardon stands at the front of the bus. "We're on another team's turf today, so I want everyone on their best behavior. Got that?"

"Yes, Coach," the team answers as a chorus.

He leans on his cane, and his eyes glide over every row, from the back to front. "But don't forget for a second we're here to kick Tamalpais High's ass something fierce. Let's do this."

We cheer and stream out. Dazed by the ride, I follow the flow from the bus to the locker room to the pool in a matter of minutes. I'm about to hop in when Zaylee skips down from the stands to meet me, wearing a tie-dyed Cal T-shirt and a sweatshirt around her waist.

She slaps my butt. I swivel around, hoping no one saw.

"You look dang cute in that tiny swimsuit," Zaylee says.

"Thanks. For coming, I mean."

"Are you kidding? This is your arena. I found a seat next to your Mom and her boyfriend. He's pretty cool."

I look up in the direction Zaylee is pointing and see Mom and Geoff. They're laughing in a way that lets me know it's even more serious than Mom's been letting on. Guess we're both moving on from Dad.

Zaylee gives me a peck on the lips. "I'd say good luck, but you don't need it."

Reardon's voice interrupts us. "Last chance to use the facilities before game time."

"Can't ignore that," I tell Zaylee and hustle into the locker room. There are few things more horrific than having to take a leak mid-game.

Declan had the same idea because we end up next to each other at the urinals.

"You ready to smash it, Coleman?" He reaches out the hand that isn't steadying his stream to punch fists with me.

I meet his fist with my own. "You know it."

"Saw your fan," Declan says. "You were telling the truth about having a senior chick."

Can't we just focus on pissing?

Declan flushes and bounds out of the locker room, yelling, "Tamalpais sucks! Go, Yellowjackets!" Somehow, I don't think this is the "best behavior" Coach Reardon had in mind.

Before I know it, we're all in the water, and the game is about to start. As the whistle blows, I take a last look at Zaylee in her seat with Mom and Geoff. Can't let my VIPs down.

Getting headbutted by opposing players, the sensation of water filling my mouth and nostrils, swimming for dear life and emerging breathless at the other end of the pool, the loud smack of my hand on the ball—these past months have transformed me into a polo player. Weirdly, Declan and I have become kind of a power duo in the pool, and I assist two spectacular goals.

The second half is a blur. Tamalpais scores on us a few times, tying things up, but by the end, we get ahead again to the tune of three consecutive goals. The final whistle blows, and our guys start shouting in triumph. My chest is empty of all air and burns like someone poured scalding tea across my insides.

Declan swims over. "Sweet game, Coleman," he says before playfully dunking me and holding me underwater for a few seconds. "Yellowjackets rule!" I hear him yell as I emerge from the water, spitting and grinning.

Hoisting myself over the pool's edge, dripping everywhere, I'm exhausted but elated. Mom and Geoff are walking down from the bleachers to greet me, with Zaylee close behind.

"Zack was incredible, wasn't he, Maggie?" Zaylee asks, smiling broadly.

"He sure was." Mom tosses her hair back and adjusts her sunglasses, making her look almost glamorous. I suddenly realize that everyone deserves someone who makes them feel wanted; Geoff does that for her.

"Nice work out there, Zack," Geoff says, offering his hand.

"Thanks, man." Geoff's got a firm grip.

"I mean, I knew you were going to be good," Zaylee says, "but I wasn't expecting a polo champion."

I stare down at the concrete. "The Yellowjackets are a strong team. I just do my part."

Just as I'm wrapping my towel around my waist and removing my cap, Tony struts by. He shoves a wet shoulder against mine as he passes, knocking me off balance.

"Hey Coleman," he says with his back to me. "Next time, try showing your lady friend some passing instead of show-boating the whole game."

Talk about timing. I'd been so high on praise from my cheering squad that I forgot guys like Tony can get real pissy when they don't get the ball enough.

I raise my hand. "Hey, Tony, wait up."

Mom bats my arm down. "Zack, there will always be people who believe they deserve the glory instead of you," she says. "It's the same in academia."

After giving Mom a quick hug and Geoff another firm handshake, I explain it's time to head back to the locker room.

Zaylee wipes away a drop of water trickling slowly down my nose; I appreciate the possessive gesture. "I'll wait around and give the winner a ride back," she says.

Score. A ride is a treat. My fellow Yellowjackets will be cramped into a stinky bus full of machismo and exhaustion while I'm chilling with my girlfriend. Looks like my lucky day all around.

We hit the Golden Gate Bridge, and the sun is peeking through the cloud cover like slivers of golden glass. Zaylee's got our favorite Third Eye Blind song cranked. Those "doo doo doos" get stuck in my head.

"Today was the best I've felt in a while," I admit to Zaylee. "Even assholes like Tony can't get me down." After the chaos of the past few weeks, normal feels like bliss. No brooding about Matthias—just basking in the utter flawless-ness of the moment.

"You're coming into your own," Zaylee says, flashing a

smile that makes me want to save every rainforest out there. "It's a glorious thing to behold."

Her words course through me like warm honey. "You know what? The idea of this 'Semi-Charmed Life' song sort of makes sense to me right now."

Zaylee tosses her head back and laughs. "Or maybe it's just a catchy song."

"Maybe." Outside the window, a pair of seagulls swoop on invisible gusts of Bay Area breeze.

Still, even a charmed life has a way of switching things up without warning, so I've got to keep my guard up. But right now, I'd rather just sing along with the "doo doo doos" and cruise.

THIRTY-FOUR
HIDDEN HEARTS

Zaylee deposits me at home with a lengthy kiss. "Get some rest, champion," she whispers into my ear. "And call me tomorrow."

"Promise."

I hop out of the car and through the courtyard, feeling unstoppable. Once inside, I grab some Ruffles from the cupboard and sit at the island, basking in the post-win glow. Mom's door is closed so I figure she's napping after her drive back.

Then I see it: a brown package decorated with kooky ballpoint pen designs straight out of the '70s. Mom brought the mail in, so she's seen the New Mexico address. It's Silas with another special delivery designed to baffle his son.

On my bed, a bag of greasy chips at my side, I gingerly open the package; for some reason, I don't want to mess up his drawings of "Kilroy was here" and Felix the Cat. Out slides a glossy book with *Santa Fe Emerging Poets Collection* in fancy writing on top of a black and white photograph of a Pueblo community. The back blurb reads, "This journal is a collection of eclectic poetry in a variety of styles by some of Santa Fe and the surrounding area's most exciting voices."

Huh?

Tucked inside the *Santa Fe Emerging Poets Collection* is a postcard with drawings of churches, conquistadors, and cattle ranchers, exclaiming, "Greetings from New Mexico, Land of Enchantment." I flip it over and greedily absorb the message.

Dearest Zack,

I've been waiting to share my poetry with you until after I'd had some real success. Ego? I suppose. The most I've got to show for myself are the poems in this journal. It's not The Paris Review, *but it's hoity-toity and hard to get accepted, so I'm damn proud they published three of mine. You don't have to read the whole thing (though some of the other poets are astonishingly good). Mine are on pages 23, 77, and 104. You're in every word, Zack. See if you can find yourself. I'm through hiding, and ready to talk the next time your mother calls.*

All of my love and hope,
Your flawed father

"Classic Dad," I say to no one.

So he's through hiding and ready to talk? We'll see. For the past two years, he's kept in touch with my mother behind my back while I've been an oblivious dipshit, going about my stupid teenage life without a clue.

I sniff the book; it smells of glue, clean and untouched. I flip through its crisp pages, eventually landing on his first poem, "Harebrained."

More and more, I've come to regret
All the moments that don't
Reintroduce me to you, improved, if not perfected

Gaping holes in behavior made smaller
And mistakes set in stone
Reality ran riot, and I must atone
End a period of banishment
Terrible yet necessary
Zero chance of forgiveness
And it serves me right
Caring for others was never my strength
Harebrained animal, I am
Always bouncing between passions
Rarely responsible
Youth is elusive, but I chase it still
So, I write from my adobe hut
In a town you do not know
Later and later into the warm night
A prisoner of pathos
Succumbing to a lifetime at your service

So what if the poem is dripping with what I once heard Mom call "your father's narcissistic self-pity?" It's also full of regret and kind of apologetic, and it touched me. I didn't know Dad could write like that.

Wait, now I see the trick. Like that drawing of an old lady with a hook nose who reveals herself to be a beautiful woman in a shawl if you stare long enough: M A R G A R E T Z A C H A R Y S I L A S.

We're all in there. Very clever.

Through the wall, I hear Mom turn on the TV. Ignoring the sitcom laughter, I skip ahead to Page 77, hungry for the next puzzle. It's a shorter piece called "Testing Site."

Test me
To see what answers the hills hold
Whether they pass or fail

Browned and ruined, green and lush
Weather, there is even a difference
Between a fall and a rise
Rain and sun
Yesterdays and tomorrows

In English, Mrs. Garcia told us we should try and uncover layers of truth in poetry, to scratch beneath the superficial and "gaze into a poem's hidden heart." But what if there is no deeper meaning? What if a poem is only screwing around with words? Like Dad screwed with our lives when he ran off to New Mexico to follow his fantasy. The guy was so up his ass he didn't even make it to my eighth-grade graduation.

"What the fuck, man?" I whisper under my breath.

I jump ahead to Dad's last poem. But before I start reading, something pulls me back to "Testing Site." I go through it again, but this time, I stop trying to imagine what Dad meant. Instead, I simply surrender to his words.

And there it is. Like a photograph developing before my eyes, I see my life appear section by section. My friendship with Matty, Dad's troubles, Matthias's troubles, my athletic drive—it's all staring at me from the page.

"Browned and ruined, green and lush." That seems to mean it doesn't matter how much you have or don't have. Situations change, people change, and we have to adapt or wither. He writes about the difference between "a fall and a rise," which might mean that landing on your ass is the first step to getting back up. I bend the spine, ready to attack the final work, "Ballad of a Stranger."

He came to me with eyes wide and afraid
I turned away, then held him near
My heart, future plans unmade

She came to me with a mind aflame, thoughts upon
  thoughts
Grazing in savannas, tumbling through technology
I held her close, then pushed her aside
Now they come to me
In daydreams and night visions
A pair of puppets, over which I was powerless
To provide a thing
Of value
Of goodness

A pair of puppets, is that how he sees us? Playthings to control and then abandon when he loses interest. Dad once told me about this Carl Jung theory where everyone you encounter in a dream is actually you. Maybe it's the same in poems, except I'm pretty sure I'm the wide-eyed baby at the beginning, and Mom is the one with the "mind aflame." He always told me she was the most intelligent person he'd ever met.

I slap the poetry collection closed, let it drop from my hand to the floor, and stretch out on the bed, nestling myself in the covers. The salt from the last Ruffles chip spreads across my tongue, making me crave another twenty to crunch away my feelings because I'm having a shitload of them.

Completely zonked, my thoughts float along in a half-dream state. From high in an imaginary sky, I trace a pair of strings connected to a puppet of my dad, the wandering poet, with a pen and a notebook in its felt hands. I move the marionette version of him around a puppet theater resembling the castle in *Mister Rogers' Neighborhood*. Only here, it's in a desert with cacti and tumbleweeds. I flop Dad from one side of the tiny box to the other. Following Jung's dream logic, it all makes perfect sense.

Another puppet appears in the wings, waiting for its grand entrance. The doll is my spitting image—Yellowjackets hoodie and all. On the other side of the stage is a puppet of my mother with curly hair and crossed arms. At first, I can't tell who's pulling her strings because of the blinding desert sun, but it turns out that I'm controlling all three of us.

Maybe Mrs. Garcia meant reading poetry reveals our *own* hidden hearts.

Back in the real world, I rustle around the bed, struggling to find a better position. Eventually, I curl into a ball with my head tucked between my knees. My eyes shut tight, and my throat constricts. A warm tear meanders down my cheek, and more follow. In my half-dream, I walk miniature Dad over to miniature me, wrap our puppet arms around each other, and understand what forgiveness might feel like.

THIRTY-FIVE
TOO WISE FOR WORDS

The vibe inside Coconut Palace is maximum chill: dim, recessed lighting and bamboo plants in every corner. Mom's excuse for bringing me to this fancy Thai restaurant was to celebrate my polo win, but I'm dubious. It's too much of an obvious olive branch, a chance to patch things up after the Matthias debacle. What she doesn't know is Dad's special delivery has me reassessing everything.

"Seeing you in your element again, even playing a different sport, that was a pleasure for me." She's nursing a glass of red wine, eyes drooping at the corners. "Geoff and I were so impressed."

"It was cool seeing you guys in the stands," I say, and take a bite of my Pad Thai. The flavor is sweet and complex, a universe away from my standard pizza-taco-burger diet.

"Oh, you barely noticed us." Mom plunges her fork into a pile of flat, brownish noodles. "You get so focused when you're playing. It was the same with wrestling. That drive is a gift, Zack."

"Moms have to say crap like that."

"Doesn't make it any less true."

"Fine, I'll take the compliment. This time."

As we eat in silence, the clanging knives and yuppie laughter seem to increase in volume.

Mom takes a deep gulp of wine. "Zaylee is so cute and polite," she says. "And most importantly, *smart*."

I rub my shoulder, suddenly hyper-aware of how sore I am since the game. "She's amazing. But once she goes away to college, she'll forget I ever existed."

"I doubt that. You're highly memorable." Mom dabs her mouth with a napkin. "So, would you say she's your *girlfriend*?"

"OK, this is officially uncomfortable," I say, squirming in my seat. "But yes, we've moved in that direction."

Mom looks away, and I pick at the leftover peanuts and bean sprouts on my plate. "What did Zaylee think of your friend Matthias?"

Booyah. Here we go. "I bet it'd make you giddy to know Zaylee hates Matty's guts."

She pushes her glass away. "Well, she does have a good head on her shoulders."

"The only reason I even *met* Zaylee is because of Matthias."

"So, they were friends once?"

I sigh. Why is she so nosey about this shit from back in the Paleolithic Period? "He used to bug her at work. I guess he liked her or something."

"Who wouldn't? But she's way out of his league."

Memories of Matthias race through my brain: the first time I saw him at school, the two of us smoking cigarettes at Gilman, our mushroom trip. "I think it's fucked that you made me divorce my best friend."

"That's pretty dramatic."

I make myself as tall as possible in my seat. "You need to know I have my own reasons for separating from Matty. Shit that has nothing to do with you or Zaylee or anyone."

Now she's the one sitting up. "I'm listening."

"Matty's not some delinquent. Guess who taught me about Harvey Milk and Angela Davis? Matthias and his family."

"I sense a 'but' coming."

My heart is pounding like a timpani drum. I need to get this off my heart and into the air. "He makes me forget who I am sometimes. I act differently when I'm with him."

Our eyes connect.

"You've always been so independent," Mom says in a soft, wistful voice.

"That's why I needed space from him—not just because you forced me to break things off. I'm figuring out who I am on my own terms."

Mom motions to the waiter passing by and points at her wine glass. "That makes two of us."

She reaches across the table and scratches my hair like I'm an eight-year-old crying because he spent his last quarter at the arcade.

"Guess you know I got some more mail from Dad."

Her eyebrows rise over her glasses like twin moons. "Well, your father's packages are distinctive."

"That's one way of putting it." The mood lightens, like when you make a joke after a melodramatic movie scene. "He sent me a journal."

"To inspire you to become a writer?"

"Not that kind of journal." I lean back, savoring the power of knowing something about him that she doesn't. "It's a poetry anthology. Dad's got three poems in it."

The waiter returns to refill her glass. "How'd they strike you?"

"Kind of pretentious, but deep. Why does he have to be this mysterious Jim Morrison-type figure all the time?"

"Well, Silas tossed aside a lot of stability to live like that."

"Tossed his family aside too."

"Yes, us too."

I push my dish away. "Matthias has wild dreams. The two of them are hella similar."

"Artistic, determined, frustrated. I see it."

I think of those puppets of my father and me in the make-believe desert—from when my subconscious morphed into *The Muppet Show* on acid.

Mom squeezes my hand; hers is cool and soft. "Give him a chance. Parents need their kid's approval as much as the other way around."

"You know what's wild? I think I'm ready to forgive Dad."

She smiles, pulls her hand away, and pats her purse.

"Well, without him, we wouldn't be in Berkeley right now having this meal, would we?"

"For real," I say while pulling my chair out from the table. "And Cali's pretty sweet. You get to become a new version of yourself here."

"You, young man, are too wise for words."

A collage of shadows and light passes through the car's interior as we pull out from the parking lot. A gang of rowdy voices blasts out of the speakers, roaring about getting knocked down and getting back up. They sound drunk to me. Then, a lonely trumpet plays a solo before the chant begins again. "That was Chumbawamba with 'Tubthumping,'" the DJ announces over the song's ending.

"That's quite a mouthful," Mom says.

"Chumba what?"

We look at each other and crack up. She turns the radio

down slowly, allowing us to fall into the gentle rhythm of the road.

My mind drifts. I'm thinking about how some people like to hear themselves talk and talk and talk. Coach Reardon with his lectures, punk lessons from Matthias, Dad quoting his beloved poets. Right now, the silence says everything. Things will be different, but they'll be OK.

THIRTY-SIX
RAINBOW'S END

It's nearly Valentine's Day, and I'm stoked to announce that Zaylee now lets me refer to her as my girlfriend. We even saw *Titanic* (which everyone is freaking out over) over winter break, which is like the antithesis of Matty's punk rock rules. Oh, and the new and improved me isn't even afraid to admit I enjoyed the movie, except that one cheesy ballad.

Even better, with a few months of steady dating under our belts, we've got a weekday routine down. Zaylee meets me after polo practice and hands over the keys.

That's right, I'm almost a licensed driver. I got my learner's permit just before New Year's. Though, to be fair, the responsibility still terrifies me. Most days, I take the easy side streets until we settle on a secluded spot to fool around while listening to Alanis Morissette or No Doubt on repeat.

Today, I'm driving aimlessly while pestering Zaylee about my least favorite topic: our future together. "When do you start hearing from colleges so you can leave this city behind and forget me?"

She snorts. "Guilt trip, much? You sound like my parents."

"Nah, your parents are chill."

It's true. As promised, Zaylee invited me over to meet her mom and dad for the holidays. We had a feast and watched *Jingle All the Way* with Arnold Schwarzenegger.

Unsurprisingly, her family is a cozy unit with a hundred and one inside jokes. I did my best to laugh at the right times and be a stellar boyfriend. Overall, I think I made a decent impression.

"It seemed like they liked me," I say, slowing down over a speed bump.

"As if, Zack. Everyone likes you."

Not everyone. Matthias's voice spitting "fucking poseur" echoes in my mind.

A song called "Beautiful Disaster" comes on the radio, and soon we're rocking out and singing along at the top of our lungs. It starts out as mellow reggae before morphing into crunchy rock and back. It's kind of like life. You're cruising along, lost in a rhythm, when another scoops you up and switches the whole plan.

"Look, I'm stuck in boring Catholic school all week," Zaylee says, hoisting her green Converse sneakers onto the glove compartment. "Take me somewhere exciting, Mr. Driver-in-Training."

I flip the blinker on. "Your wish is my command."

She places a hand on my thigh, which is somewhat distracting when attempting a U-turn, but I somehow pull off the maneuver. We wind our way through city streets—because I'm nowhere near confident on the freeway yet—so it takes eons to reach our destination. That's right, Telegraph Avenue, somewhere *I* can be the tour guide. Once we're close, I find a parking spot a few blocks away from the action and we huff it.

As we stroll arm in arm, Zaylee fills me in on a presentation her Environmental Club gave to the middle school kids. She's so pumped that even *I'm* starting to feel inspired to recycle.

"Why does everything you do have to be meaningful and help the world?" I ask. "It makes me feel inadequate."

"We can talk about water polo if you want—or WWF." Zaylee stops short, dashes behind my back, and puts me in a fake headlock.

"I never should have revealed my childhood professional wrestling obsession," I say, sliding out from beneath her slim arm. "Did I tell you I looked up Angela Davis on the internet? She's a legend."

Zaylee fake slaps my wrist. "No, you certainly did *not*. Check out Zack getting all radicalized. I like it. Berkeley is rubbing off on you."

"Guess so." Suddenly, inspiration hits. "Wait, have you ever been to Amoeba?"

She stares at me like I named an obscure island off the coast of Papua New Guinea. "Have I been *where*?"

"Amoeba is a record store, but way more. Let me show you."

Zaylee places her arm around my shoulders, and I lean into her. I'm so caught up in the feeling of us that I hardly notice a group of skaters doing jumps off the curb a block ahead. Baggy jeans cinched below their butts, bulky blue and red sweatshirts, clanging wallet chains—kids like this used to be wallpaper to me. Not anymore.

As we approach, I start to make out their forms: a girl, a short, dark-haired guy, and a beanpole in ginormous pants, even by skater standards. Tina. Rob. And, of course, Matthias. I feel my back stiffen. My girlfriend and I are on a crash course for my old life.

"Watch this," Rob shouts and attempts a kick-flip far

exceeding his abilities. I feel like I'm in one of those lucid dreams, where everything is familiar, yet somehow totally absurd.

The skaters don't clear the way, so I steer us left to avoid bumping into them. They don't seem to recognize me. Zaylee doesn't pay them any mind, her eyes glued to the sidewalk as she lectures passionately about water conservation. Maybe, if we speed up—

Then, as if by magnetism, Matthias and I look up simultaneously. He brushes his bangs back, and our eyes connect. The hair is longer in front, shaved in the back, and bleached bright blonde with blue streaks, but he's still the same Matty. And I'm still Dr. Z, whoever that is.

He says nothing, and neither do I, but we're communicating. In the space of a few seconds, I read a spectrum of emotions: surprise, betrayal, anger. Above all, I see a hell of a lot of loneliness.

No time to think. Just go for the win.

Without words, I try to convey to Matthias how fucking sorry I am for what happened to our friendship, that we were blood brothers. It's some heavy emotion to cram into a stare-off, but I give it my best shot. Matty's eyes look like they're starting to water. My telepathy is working; he's receiving the transmission.

Then he breaks my gaze and boom, the spell is broken.

Zaylee and I walk on, and I try to act like nothing happened. We pass beneath a tree as a careless breeze rustles its leaves, sending a lengthy shiver up my neck. There may be such a thing as a California winter, after all.

Suddenly, I hear Matthias's voice behind us yelling, "Hey!"

I turn around on the sly. Matty is looking in our direction, but he averts his eyes.

"Peep this old-school Neil Blender 50-50 grind," he

announces to Tina and Rob and hops onto a city bench, skimming the edge before hitting the ground—legs crouched and arms outstretched.

I'm no expert, but Matty looked wobbly just now. Maybe he's rusty after months of forced recuperation. Or perhaps he's just a decent high school street skater who isn't as ready to turn pro as he wants everyone to believe. Another layer of magic is peeling away, revealing the reality that Matty is only a kid, just like me.

Once we're out of earshot, I consider telling Zaylee who I just saw, but what's the point? That was a secret moment between blood brothers. Instead, I drag her along, quickening the pace so the houses and foliage blur. Soon, we're passing surplus stores and steaming food kiosks until we're deep in the heart of the Avenue. I point to a large, looming building: Amoeba Records. "There it is," I proclaim. "The end of the rainbow."

"What makes this place so incredible again?"

"There are plenty of music stores," I reply. "Amoeba is an experience."

We pass through security, and my heart starts to race like it did back when Matthias shoved that contraband into his waistband. Like so many of my experiences with him, we narrowly escaped a shitshow supreme. I rub a sweaty palm across my forehead at the memory.

Luckily, Zaylee is here to rescue me from my junkyard of bad thoughts. I watch as she soaks up the sights and sounds of the store: the infinite rows of red-stickered CDs and records, colorful posters sparring for wall space, and the ear-splitting sound system daring patrons to stay.

"This place is like a colossal music supermarket," she says. "It's intimidating."

"What are you looking for?" I ask in my best connoisseur voice. "Punk, alternative rock, pop?"

She crosses her arms. "You know me. If I like a song, I like it."

"Songs are great," I say, thumbing through a bin and stopping on a record by Daft Punk. "But certain albums you have to experience from start to finish, like a movie for your mind."

All at once, I have an idea. After a quick dash to the hip-hop section, I return with A Tribe Called Quest's *Beats, Rhymes and Life* in my hand. "You need to hear this," I tell her. "It's a psychedelic musical trip."

Zaylee groans.

"*Without* the drugs," I sputter. "I can't even imagine doing that stupid bullshit again." Considering Matthias, Dad, and everything I've learned about bipolar disorder, I'm in no hurry to mess with my chemical balance.

"Well, I like that artwork," Zaylee says, grabbing the album from me.

"Matthias turned me onto Tribe. They're the absolute shiznit. He's the one who brought me to Amoeba for the first time."

"You two were mad close," she says, without looking up from the cartoon cover. "I wasn't as understanding as I could have been—as your girlfriend."

There's that magic word. "It's OK. You were just looking out for me."

"Look, I've had challenging friendships," Zaylee says, handing me back the CD. "There was this girl named Ellie freshman year I had to cut things off with."

"Let me guess. You guys took a bunch of drugs and got in trouble?"

Zaylee gives me a stop-screwing-around look. "We hung out nonstop until I heard her make a shitty racist comment about our school janitor. After that, I couldn't stay friends with her."

Her story hits me like a polo ball to the face. "I feel like an idiot."

"You're far from an idiot," she says. "That's how life goes. We learn about ourselves from who we choose to spend time with."

We shuffle down the aisle with no particular destination, just browsing the bins and being a couple in public, a thrill unto itself. When we reach the punk section, I pick up *Stranger Than Fiction* by Bad Religion. "Now this album may legitimately change your perspective about politics, organized religion, everything," I say.

"That's some serious praise for a punk band."

I flip the CD over to reveal a figure in a hazmat suit. "Punk, yes. But there's a lot going on beneath the surface."

She slips a hand beneath my shirt and rubs my chest. "Just like you. Layers upon layers."

I lean down and put my lips on hers, not concerned about anything except this day, this kiss, this exact point in time we're sharing. After I pull myself from her, I start pointing out song titles on the Bad Religion back cover, but I've lost Zaylee's attention. She's poring over CDs on her own, each a doorway into another life, another future with or without me.

THANK YOU FOR READING

——

Did you enjoy this book?

We invite you to leave a review at your favorite book site, such as Goodreads, Amazon, Barnes & Noble, etc.

DID YOU KNOW THAT LEAVING A REVIEW...

- Helps other readers find books they may enjoy.
- Gives you a chance to let your voice be heard.
- Gives authors recognition for their hard work.
- Doesn't have to be long. A sentence or two about why you liked the book will do.

——

Don't miss your next favorite book!
Join the Fire & Ice YA Books newsletter today!
www.fireandiceya.com/mail.html

ABOUT THE AUTHOR

Ari Rosenschein is a Seattle-based author who grew up in the Bay Area. Books and records were a source of childhood solace, leading Ari to a teaching career and decades of writing, recording, and performing music. Along the way, he earned a Grammy shortlist spot, landed film and TV placements, and co-wrote the 2006 John Lennon Songwriting Contest Song of the Year.

In his writing, Ari combines these twin passions. *Coasting*, his debut short story collection, was praised by *Newfound Journal* as "introducing us to new West Coast archetypes who follow the tradition of California Dreaming into the 21st century."

Dr. Z and Matty Take Telegraph is his first young adult novel.

Official Site: www.arirosenschein.com

f facebook.com/arirosenscheinauthor
⊙ instagram.com/arirosenschein

Made in United States
Troutdale, OR
05/08/2024

19729243R00136